Nick was such good company.

Helen doubted anyone could be bored in his presence, but underneath there was something else—an awareness between them, tinged with excitement, a dangerous awareness with strong sexual undertones that, to Helen, was almost alien.

Her relationship with Richard was quiet, safe, with no emotional fireworks and she knew Nick had been quick to question its predictability. But it was what she wanted and now, when it was almost within her grasp, Nick had come along and forced her to examine it, even if only for a second.

D0609016

Laura MacDonald lives in the Isle of Wight. She is married and has a grown-up family. She has enjoyed writing fiction since she was a child, but for several years she worked for members of the medical profession, both in pharmacy and in general practice. Her daughter is a nurse and has helped with the research for Laura's medical stories.

Recent titles by the same author:

FORSAKING ALL OTHERS*
FROM THIS DAY FORWARD*
TO HAVE AND TO HOLD*
*_Matchmaker_ quartet

TO LOVE
AND TO CHERISH

BY
LAURA MACDONALD

MILLS & BOON®

*First published in Great Britain 1998
Harlequin Mills & Boon Limited,
Eton House, 18-24 Paradise Road, Richmond, Surrey TW9 1SR*

© Laura MacDonald 1998

ISBN 0 263 81240 5

*Set in Times Roman 10½ on 12 pt.
03-9810-50159-D*

*Printed and bound in Norway
by AiT Trondheim AS, Trondheim*

CHAPTER ONE

'WHO's the best man, for heaven's sake? Wow, what a hunk!'

'Dot, please try and control yourself.' Helen turned to take a glass of sherry from one of the waiters but she was forced to suppress a smile at her friend's open enthusiasm.

'But who is he? Where did he come from?' Dot quite obviously had no intention of letting the matter drop. 'I haven't seen him around here before. If I had I would have remembered—we don't get too many Mel Gibson look-alikes at the Shalbrooke.'

'Kate said he was a friend of Jonathan's,' said Helen, with a quick glance to the far end of the hotel dining room where the top-table guests were sorting out who should sit where. 'I think she said they worked abroad together for the Voluntary Services.'

'I wonder how many more there are,' said Dot with a sigh.

'What do you mean?' Helen took a sip of her sherry.

'Well, when Jon Hammond arrived I didn't think there could be too many around like him.'

'What about Norman Westfield?' Helen chuckled.

'What *about* Norman Westfield?' Dot wrinkled her nose.

'He adores you,' protested Helen.

'That may well be,' said Dot briskly. 'But Mel Gibson he ain't.'

'Probably not...' Helen allowed her gaze to flicker

back to the best man. He certainly was very good-looking, in a film-starrish sort of way. Not her type, though—she preferred her men a little more mature-looking and sort of dependable, while this one—this friend of Jonathan's—looked a bit devil-may-care.

As if he'd sensed her gaze on him, he chose that moment to look up and their eyes met and held—his becoming slightly quizzical as if perhaps he felt he should know her.

Slightly flustered at the directness of his stare, Helen looked away. She was saved from further embarrassment as the reception got under way and she and Dot took their places at one of the large round tables.

It had been all weddings that year, Helen thought later during the speeches when the meal was over and she allowed her mind to wander back over the preceding months. First there had been Georgina and Andrew Merrick who worked with Helen at the Shalbrooke hospital and who had remarried following their divorce—that had been at Easter.

Then, only last month, in September, Helen's cousin's daughter, Siobhan, had married her fellow paramedic, Dave Morey. That wedding had taken place in Ireland and Helen had travelled to County Cork for the full nuptial mass. And now here was her childhood friend, Kate Chapman, marrying Jonathan Hammond, a locum who was standing in for one of Kate's partners at the practice where she was a GP.

Kate looked radiant in a plain dress of ivory satin with fresh flowers in her dark hair. Helen watched her as she gazed up adoringly at the man who had quite literally swept her off her feet in a whirlwind romance, and she had to fight a sudden stab of envy, not because she harboured any such feelings about Jon Hammond herself—

she had Richard, after all—but for the sheer heady romance of it all.

'Ladies and Gentleman, I give you the best man—Mr Nick Sawyer.'

The toastmaster stood back and Jon Hammond's friend rose. Helen turned to watch him and saw there was no trace of nerves as he surveyed the gathering. His gaze spanned the room again and, disconcertingly, came to rest for the briefest of moments on herself before he turned to the bride and groom.

His speech was competent and witty, just as she had anticipated it would be, and he soon evoked gales of laughter from the guests as he recalled several incidents from his and Jon's college days and later from their times together on various bush stations and far-flung outposts.

It was Helen's chance to study him, unobserved, as he could hardly stare at her throughout his speech, without giving rise to speculation. What Dot Sharman had said was true—he really was very good-looking—but Helen had the feeling he knew it. He brimmed with confidence and self-assurance, his hazel eyes glittering with amusement as he moved swiftly from one story to another.

Then, with the speeches over, the cake cut and yet more photographs taken, the guests began to leave their tables and to drift outside onto the hotel terrace and into the grounds, the lawns of which ran right down to the shores of the Solent.

'Your turn next, Helen?' Looking up quickly, Helen found Georgina Merrick at her elbow.

'Oh, I don't know about that.' Helen laughed. 'I was just thinking—I guess three weddings in a year are quite enough for Shalbrooke.'

'I'm sure there would be room for another,' said Georgina. Glancing around, she said, 'So, where is Richard? I saw him earlier at the church...'

'He drew the short straw today,' said Helen ruefully. 'He's on call.'

'Well I suppose someone had to be,' said Georgina, 'with two out of four GPs out of action. Are they going away?'

'Only for a couple of nights,' said Helen. 'They'll probably have a proper honeymoon later when Paul Wooldridge gets back from his sabbatical, but at the moment, I don't think they could be spared from the practice.' She stood up. 'I think I'm going to get a breath of fresh air, Georgina. Are you coming?'

'I need the loo first,' Georgina replied, glancing over her shoulder, 'but I'll join you in a bit.'

'All right.' Helen nodded and began to make her way to the tall French windows behind the top table.

It had been a glorious day with the depth of blue in the sky that only October brought. The fresh sea air from the Solent was crisp and bracing, but the breeze that rippled through the copper beeches that lined the drive and stirred the gold of a belt of sycamores was only slight and with barely a chill about it. Helen stood on the terrace and took several deep breaths.

'I thought I might find you out here.' The voice was deep, with just a hint of humour in it. She knew who it was even before she turned.

'Kate tells me you are her best friend,' he went on, not giving her the chance to even wonder what she should say.

'We certainly go back a long way,' she agreed.

'To school-days I understand.' The dark eyebrows were raised.

'Yes, we were both at school here on the Isle of Wight,' Helen said, and added, 'A bit like you and Jon I suppose.'

'Not quite. We met at medical school then went into the VSO at the same time.' He paused. 'Shall we walk for a while—stretch our legs?'

Helen glanced over her shoulder but there was no sign of Georgina or Dot so she nodded and they moved across the terrace and down the steps onto the lawns.

'So, are you still with the VSO?' she asked, throwing him a curious glance.

He shook his head. 'Not at the moment, no. I did a long spell in India then went up into the hill country around Afghanistan and into Nepal. I felt I needed a break so I came home to Norfolk. Like Jon, I've been doing a bit of locum work.'

'In general practice?' she asked.

'No, hospital work.' He paused and suddenly, as they walked, their feet making no sound on the soft velvet of the grass, he said, 'How about you? Are you a doctor, like Kate?'

'Heavens, no,' said Helen with a short laugh. 'I'm a nurse.'

'Ah, I thought as much. Where do you work?'

'I'm at the Shalbrooke.'

'Isn't that the hospital next door to Kate's group practice…now what is that called?' He frowned.

'The Fleetwood Centre—yes, that's the one.' Helen nodded.

'What department are you?'

'Accident and Emergency,' she replied.

'That's a coincidence.' He gave a short laugh. 'That's where I am in Norwich at the moment. Locum Casualty

Officer—but, like I say, it's only a temporary post.' He paused. 'So, are you a staff nurse?'

'No, Senior Sister.'

'I'm impressed.' A teasing note had crept into his voice. Growing serious again, he went on, 'I think it's time we introduced ourselves—Nick Sawyer.' He held out his hand while they walked and when Helen responded she felt hers grasped in a firm strong handshake.

'Helen Turner,' she replied.

'Well, Helen I'm delighted to meet you,' he said. With a sudden sense of certainty Helen knew he meant it, just as, equally as suddenly, she became very aware of him. When she'd first set eyes on him she'd been instinctively wary of his good looks, then later of his confident, assured manner. From her own experience she knew that the two were very often companions to conceit or arrogance, but she had to admit there was no trace of either in the man who strolled at her side.

'Kate tells me you recently lost your father,' he said, and there was a certain sympathy in the directness of his tone.

'Yes.' Helen swallowed and nodded. The subject still hit a raw nerve whenever it was raised. 'He had Alzheimer's. It…it was very distressing at the end. He didn't know me or anything.'

'It gets to you, doesn't it?' He paused then added, 'My father died a couple of years ago. I was in Katmandu at the time and when I came home for the funeral I couldn't accept that he was truly gone. He was always such a big man if you know what I mean—not only in his size, but in his presence. He seemed to fill a room the moment he entered it, and I couldn't accept he would no longer do that.'

'Was it a sudden death?' asked Helen curiously.

'Yes.' Nick nodded. 'A heart attack. One moment he was mowing the lawn—the next he was gone. I honestly don't know what's worse. I guess that's the best way for the person concerned, but it's a tremendous shock for those that are left. On the other hand, I dare say the trauma that you went through, seeing your father deteriorate, was pretty awful as well.'

'Yes,' Helen agreed. 'It was—pretty awful.'

'So, do you have other family?'

'A sister, but she and her family live in Scotland, and various cousins...'

'You're not married?' In the moment that followed the question it was almost as if he held his breath.

'No,' she said, 'no, I'm not married...'

'Nor I,' he said quickly. 'Never got round to it somehow, what with being abroad so much...and never having met the right person, of course.'

'Well, yes, that would play a major part, I suppose.' She laughed. While they had been talking they had walked almost in a circle and were once again facing the hotel. 'I never thought Kate would get around to it,' she said, and glanced up at the terrace as she spoke, her gaze coming to rest on Kate and Jon who were posing on the steps for yet more photographs. 'And then Jon comes along and quite suddenly that's it—Kate is head over heels in love.'

'I gather it can happen when one least expects it.'

'So they tell me,' murmured Helen.

He turned his head to look at her. 'I can't believe you don't have first-hand knowledge of that.'

'Did I say I didn't?' Helen raised her eyebrows.

'Have you?' he asked softly.

'I think, Mr Sawyer you are too inquisitive by half.' She spoke firmly but there was humour in her tone.

'Oh, please—Nick,' he said quickly. 'My friends call me Nick.'

'Am I to be counted in that number on such short acquaintance?'

'Why not? After all, I don't have any doubts we would be friends on longer acquaintance—do you?' he added.

'No,' she said quite spontaneously, 'I don't.' And she was surprised to find she really meant it. By this time they had reached the steps, where Georgina was standing with her husband, Andrew.

'Andrew, Georgina,' said Helen, 'have you met Nick Sawyer?'

They both shook their heads and introductions followed. Turning to Andrew, Helen said, 'Nick is working in A and E in a hospital in Norwich at the moment.' For Nick's benefit she said, 'Andrew is our casualty officer at the Shalbrooke.'

'Is that so?' Interest flickered in Nick Sawyer's hazel eyes.

'Not for much longer.' Andrew laughed. 'I'm shortly taking up a post in Southampton, hopefully another step closer to my consultancy.' He paused. 'How about you?'

'Oh, mine is only a temporary locum post,' said Nick.

'Well, if you find yourself out of a job, there'll be one going at the Shalbrooke when I go,' said Andrew. As he spoke Helen looked up sharply, suddenly finding the idea of Nick Sawyer working on her unit somehow disturbing but at the same time curiously exciting. She dismissed the idea almost before it had formed. It was so improbable that it was hardly worth contemplating.

'I might just consider that,' said Nick, to her surprise. 'I quite fancy the idea of living on an island.'

'You can't beat it,' said Andrew.

'Won't you have to move to the mainland when you are at Southampton?' asked Nick.

Andrew shook his head. 'No way. I shall commute. Then, hopefully, when I have my consultancy I will be able to obtain another position here on the Island.'

A sudden shout from the terrace made them all turn. 'Kate and Jon are just leaving!'

Together with the rest of the guests, they made their way around the hotel to the forecourt where a vintage Rolls Royce was drawn up at the main entrance. There was a further shout as Jon and Kate appeared, a moment of laughter and confusion, a flurry of confetti and good-byes. As Kate moved towards the car her bouquet sailed through the air and was neatly caught by an unsuspecting Helen. There followed a round of spontaneous applause, more laughter and a degree of speculation.

'Your turn next, Helen.'

'When's it to be?'

'Well, well.' This last was from Nick who stood close beside her, so close she caught the scent of his after-shave.

Dot called from the far side of the courtyard, 'Does Richard know about this, Helen?'

In the laughter that followed Helen felt her cheeks suddenly burn as for that brief moment she was the focus of everyone's attention.

'And who,' murmured Nick in her ear, 'is Richard?'

'Talk of the devil,' called someone else as a Volvo swept up the drive, crunched to a halt behind the Rolls and a familiar, slightly stocky figure got out.

'That's Richard,' said Helen. 'He's Kate's partner.'

'And?' Again the eyebrows raised maddeningly.

'What do you mean—and?' Helen frowned, watching as Richard went across to the Rolls and kissed Kate.

'Well, there must be some other significance to you personally if you take into account the comments that were made when you caught those flowers.'

'Yes, I suppose there is.' Helen paused. 'These people obviously think it's high time that Richard and I tied the knot as well.'

'Ah,' he said knowingly, and then, moving so that he was able to look straight into her eyes, he said, 'And what about you—is that what you think as well?'

'It would seem to be the next logical move,' said Helen. 'We've been…seeing each other for a long time now.'

There was a further flurry of excitement as the Rolls Royce drew away—shouting, waving, the clatter of tin cans tied to the bumper and a cacophony of car hooters.

'So, unlike Kate's, yours was not a heady romance where you were swept off your feet and fell head over heels in love?' Nick persisted.

'Well, no, not exactly,' Helen admitted, then added defensively, 'But that's not to say it means any less. Richard and I have known each other for a very long time. We are very…very…'

'Yes?' said Nick earnestly. 'Very what?'

'Very comfortable together,' replied Helen firmly as Richard, with a final wave to the retreating Rolls, turned and began to walk towards them.

'Ah—comfortable,' said Nick.

'There's nothing wrong with comfortable,' said Helen. She spoke sharply but out of the corner of her mouth.

'Absolutely not,' Nick agreed.

'Hello, old thing,' said Richard as he reached her side. 'Sorry I had to abandon you back there. But, never mind, I'm here now. What's that you've got there—Kate's flowers?'

'Yes, Richard…'

'That's nice. For Harry's grave, are they? That was kind of her.'

Helen opened her mouth to correct him, then, catching Nick Sawyer's eye and sensing his suppressed amusement, she closed it again.

'Georgina, would you go to Treatment Room One, please, and, Denny, you and Dot deal with the "walking wounded" this morning.' It was a week after Kate's wedding, and on that particular morning the reception area of A and E at the Shalbrooke was packed. There had been two road traffic accidents, with several victims suffering from multiple injuries, and if that wasn't enough there seemed to be a heavier than usual number of patients with complaints of a lesser degree.

Wearily Helen followed Dot down the passage to one of the cubicles where a young man with severe stomach cramps was lying on the bed.

'So, when did these pains start?' asked Helen, as Dot proceeded to check the man's temperature and blood pressure.

'Last night,' the man muttered, drawing up his knees as another bout of pain racked his body.

'Can you tell me exactly where the pain is?' asked Helen. 'Is it more to one side of your stomach than the other?'

'Most of the time it's right in the middle,' gasped the man, 'but sometimes it feels very sore…just here.' He indicated his right side.

'Any diarrhoea or sickness?'

'I was sick once this morning.'

'Right,' said Helen briskly. 'When Nurse has taken a few details we'll send the doctor along to see you. All right, Nurse?' Dot nodded and for the first time that morning Helen noticed that she looked pale and rather strained.

Thoughtfully Helen made her way back to the nurses' station where she had no further time to even consider what might be ailing Dot Sharman. When at last the crowd of patients had cleared a little, Elliot Ferguson, the nursing manager, called her into his office.

'All well, Helen?' he asked, peering at her over the top of his glasses and then—without waiting for an answer—carrying on with what he was saying.

Elliot always did that and Helen found herself wondering quite what he would do if she'd said that, no, everything wasn't all right and she had some horrendous problem that only he could solve. She never did, of course, not because she didn't have any problems—there were always plenty of those on the busy A and E unit— but because she knew Elliot relied on her to keep things running smoothly.

'Helen, sit down, please. I've had details of a medical conference that is being held in London at the end of this month. It's called "Medicine in the Millennium" and management is recommending that we send a representative from this hospital as usual. This time it's the turn of this department.'

'And you want me to say who I can spare…is that it?' Helen rolled her eyes.

'Actually—' Elliot began, but it was Helen's turn to prevent him from speaking.

'I really don't know,' she went on. 'I presume you're talking nursing staff here…so I guess it will have to be one of the staff nurses because Stephanie has some holiday coming up so she won't be keen to go, Denise is busy renovating the house she and Ian have bought, and Georgina—'

'Actually,' Elliot said again, 'I was thinking of you.'

'Me?' Helen stopped in mid-sentence and stared at him.

'Yes. Is that so improbable?'

'Oh, I couldn't, Elliot,' she said quickly. 'Really, I couldn't.'

'Why not?'

'Well...well...it's so busy here. Jill is still on maternity leave and...and...'

'And what?'

Helen shrugged helplessly.

'I think it might do you good,' said Elliot. 'You always used to enjoy courses, Helen.'

'I know.' She nodded. 'But that was before...before...' She trailed off.

'Before you had your dad to care for.' Elliot finished the sentence for her. 'That was a few months ago now, Helen and you haven't been anywhere since.'

'I went to Ireland for Siobhan's wedding,' she protested weakly.

'Just for a weekend. You could do with a break, Helen.'

'I'm not really in the mood for holidays.'

'Well, this could be a little more than a holiday. The conference is at a very good hotel near Hyde Park so you would be very comfortable, you'd have a change of scenery, which would provide the break I think you need, and the conference itself sounds as if it could be extremely interesting. According to the prospectus...' Elliot passed a wad of leaflets over the desk to Helen '...one of the subjects they are discussing is alternative medicine which, you must admit, has always fascinated you, and another is identifying the cause of a complaint rather than simply treating the symptoms. Again, something I know you find interesting.'

'Keep on like this and you'll convince me.' Helen laughed and began glancing through the leaflets.

'Good,' said Elliot briskly, 'because that is the whole object of the exercise. Take the leaflets home tonight, Helen, give it some thought, then let me know in the morning what you decide.'

'No sense of urgency, then?' Helen pulled a face. 'But seriously, Elliot, what about shifts and staff rotas?'

'We'll manage,' he said firmly. 'We're only talking about a week for heaven's sake. If we can't sort out some cover for you for that long then it's a pretty poor show.'

'I should go,' said Dot when Helen returned to the nurses' station and told her and Georgina what Elliot had proposed. 'It'll do you good.'

'It won't be all holiday,' protested Helen.

'It'll be a change of air, Helen,' said Georgina. 'It's what you need after all that's happened recently.'

'Yes,' agreed Dot, adding, 'and it'll get you away from here for a while.'

There was something in the way she said it that caused Helen to look at her more closely, and while Georgina hurried back to the treatment room to cope with a suspected coronary that had just come in she said, 'Is everything all right, Dot?'

'Yes, I suppose so,' Dot sighed.

'You look a bit under the weather this morning.'

'Wrong time of the month, that's all,' said Dot. 'I had to laugh when that young chap was going on about his stomach cramps because at that particular moment my stomach was hurting so much I could have cheerfully curled up on the bed next to him.'

Helen smiled then said, 'What was the outcome with him?'

'Appendicitis,' said Dot. 'They took him up to Men's Surgical.'

'So, what about your stomach cramps—what did you do about those?'

'Two paracetamol, a cup of canteen tea and grin and bear it.'

'You don't think a chat with your GP might be overdue?' asked Helen gently. 'I seem to recall this happens most months now.'

'No.' Dot waved her hand dismissively. 'It's just one of those things. You've just got to get on with it, haven't you?' Not waiting for a reply, she went on, 'Are you going to go, then? To this conference, I mean?'

'I'm not sure,' Helen replied. 'I haven't really decided yet.'

'Well, I think you should,' said Dot firmly. 'Like we said, it'll do you good.'

Maybe they are all right, thought Helen as she watched Dot hurry back to the cubicles. Maybe she did need a break from routine, a change of scene. When she thought about it, it had been a long time since she'd done anything different. When her father had been alive the opportunity hadn't arisen, of course, and even after his death she had been content to jog along in the same old way. Just lately, however, she'd felt a little unsettled, restless even, as if she had suddenly realised there could be more to life.

Casting her mind back, she tried to work out when she had started to feel like that, and to her surprise she realised that her restless mood seemed to stem from

Kate's wedding day. Before then she had been reasonably happy. So why should Kate getting married have upset her equilibrium? Was it that she was envious, that deep down she wanted Richard and herself to finally settle down? Or could it have something to do with the amusement in a certain pair of hazel eyes that had teased and charmed her?

She dismissed the thought as soon as it entered her head. That was ridiculous. Her restless mood had nothing whatsoever to do with having met Nick Sawyer. The fact that he kept entering her mind at the most inopportune moments was neither here nor there. He had been pleasant, certainly, and she had liked him, but that's all there was to it. She would probably never be likely to set eyes on him again, anyway. He was working in Norwich, which was a fair distance from the Isle of Wight, and later, no doubt, he would go back to his VSO work—to some far-flung village high in the Himalayas.

No, there was no point in giving him another thought. It was a pity she couldn't dismiss her feelings of restlessness in the same way.

CHAPTER TWO

HELEN travelled up to town by train, after crossing the Solent by the catamaran ferry. She then checked into a fourth-floor room of the hotel where the conference was being held. The room overlooked Hyde Park, resplendent in all its late October glory, and as Helen unpacked she suddenly felt glad that she had decided to come.

In the end it had been Richard who had finally convinced her that she should go, saying that the face of medicine was changing so much that it was important that those in the NHS should keep up with world advances both in technology and in pharmaceutical breakthroughs as the millennium approached.

'Won't you miss me?' she'd asked ruefully.

'But, of course,' he'd replied with a degree of amazement that she should even ask.

'Why don't you come with me?' she'd asked, not really hopeful, knowing what his reply would be.

'I can't leave the practice at the moment—much as I might like to. Besides, you are going so you'll be able to relay everything back for the benefit of the Fleetwood Centre.'

'Yes, I suppose so.' What she didn't add was that she had thought it might have been nice for the two of them to spend some time together.

But it wasn't to be and, although at first she'd felt despondent at being alone, as she made her way down to the conference hall for the welcoming session her spirits rose a little and she decided to take the advice of her friends and enjoy the break from routine.

It was as the first session of the conference was drawing to a close that Helen's attention was drawn to the back view of a fellow delegate, sitting a few rows ahead of her. There was something familiar about the set of the head, the dark hair and the glimpses of a firm jaw. In surprise she gazed at the back of the man's head, completely missing what the person on the platform was saying.

It couldn't be, she told herself firmly, the coincidence was too great. Firmly she transferred her gaze back to the platform and attempted to get her concentration under control again.

But in a matter of seconds her gaze had flickered back. Was it really that much of a coincidence after all? He was a doctor, when all was said and done, and this was a national conference.

If it was him there would probably be no avoiding him, at least not for the entire week. It would be inevitable that they would be thrown into each other's company sooner or later.

Helen wasn't sure why the prospect of that should pose any sort of problem, she was only aware that it did—that her heart had started to thump uncomfortably just at the thought of spending time with him.

On the other hand, could it be that she might be mistaken? The man was far enough away from her for there to be an element of doubt, and when she really thought about it she had only met him just the once so it was highly likely that this could be a simple case of mistaken identity.

Well, she thought, as the final member of the welcoming committee began to wind up his speech, any minute now she would know. As the delegates rose and filed out of the conference room into the hotel bar for pre-dinner drinks, the identity of the man in front as he stood up then turned to leave the hall would be a mystery no longer.

'I thought that was you!' He came across the bar and stood gazing down to where she was sitting at one of the tables, her drink before her. There was no mistaking the delighted surprise in his eyes.

'Hello, Nick.' She hoped she sounded casual. 'I saw you in the conference hall—at least I thought it was you, but I couldn't be sure.' She didn't add that when he had passed her on his way out she had averted her head, for some reason needing time to compose herself before he saw her after the shock of finding out that it was indeed him.

'Well,' he said incredulously, 'what a coincidence! Are you with anyone? May I join you?' He'd pulled up a chair and sat down opposite her almost before she had a chance to speak.

'Can I get you a drink or anything?' He was on his feet again.

'No, I'm fine, thank you,' she replied, indicating her glass of wine.

'I'll just get one for myself,' he said, the edge of excitement still in his tone. 'Don't go away.'

As if she could. Helplessly she watched him as he went to the bar, at a loss now to know just why she was feeling the way she did—a curious mixture of excitement and foreboding. He was formally dressed in a dark suit and tie and a crisp white shirt which somehow only served to accentuate his classically dark good looks. She wondered briefly how old he was and came to the slightly uncomfortable conclusion he was probably a little younger than herself.

Not that that should matter, of course. After all, what difference could it possibly make to her whether Nick Sawyer was older or younger or, come to that, even the same age as herself?

He was back almost immediately, his gaze seeking hers as soon as he turned from the bar, holding it as he crossed the floor and even after he'd sat down. For her part, Helen was disconcerted to find that she also seemed powerless to look away.

'I really can't believe you are here,' he said, taking a mouthful of his drink before setting the glass down on the table. 'I still can't get over the coincidence.'

'Is it really that improbable?' Helen found herself smiling at his obvious delight. 'I mean, we are both in the medical world, after all, and, let's face it, this is supposed to be a national conference.'

'I know.' He shrugged. 'But I still can't get over it. There was me having my arm twisted to attend—these things aren't really my cup of tea at all—and now, well, suddenly everything is looking one hundred per cent brighter.'

'Just because of me?' Helen raised one eyebrow. The gesture was intended to be sceptical but she was finding it increasingly difficult to disguise her own pleasure and at the same time was aware that, in turn, Nick Sawyer was also only too aware of that fact.

'Absolutely.' He smiled, his eyes crinkling at the corners. 'Which floor are you on?'

'The fourth,' she replied, then immediately wondered at the advisability of so readily volunteering such information.

Nick, however, seemed totally unfazed. 'I'm on the

fifth,' he replied candidly. 'Do you overlook the park?' When she nodded in reply, he went on, 'Doesn't it look glorious—all those colours? We must go over there for a walk—early morning is probably the best, don't you agree?'

'Well, yes...'

'It's a date, then. Tomorrow morning—an early morning stroll through Hyde Park.'

She opened her mouth to say something, she wasn't sure what, but he didn't give her the chance, sweeping on, 'But before that we have dinner. You *will* join me for dinner? Honestly, Helen, I really can't believe this, you know. Here was I contemplating a very lonely dinner, not yet knowing anyone here, and now...well!'

His enthusiasm was so infectious it was impossible not to be affected and a little later Helen found herself accompanying Nick into the hotel dining room. She waited while he murmured something to one of the waiters, then they found themselves being ushered to a table for two when most of the other tables were set for four, six, or even eight people.

'What news of Kate and Jon?' he asked a little later, after they were seated and awaiting their first course.

'They are both well and settling down to married life,' said Helen. 'Kate told me they enjoyed their weekend break but that it was all too short.'

'Where was it they went?' Nick frowned.

'Torquay. I understand they are planning a longer trip when Paul Wooldridge returns to the practice—that's the partner Jon has been standing in for,' she explained.

'Yes, I know.' Nick nodded. 'I remember Paul from medical school, although I didn't know him as well as I know Jon.' He paused. 'Jon was telling me that he may be looking to the Shalbrooke for employment at the end

of the year, but that what he would really like is for the
Fleetwood practice to take him on as a fifth partner.' He
paused again as the waiter arrived at their table with their
first course. 'Do you think there's any chance of that?'
he continued when the man moved away.

'I would think there's every possibility,' Helen replied
as she picked up her fork. 'The practice has grown con-
siderably in the last two years. Richard would like to
take on another partner but they can't, of course, make
any real decisions like that until Paul returns.'

'You know, Helen,' he said after a while, 'I still can't
believe we've met again under these circumstances. I
must confess that when I first saw you sitting there in
the bar I imagined that Richard would be with you.'

'No.' Helen shook her head. 'I did mention it to him
but he wasn't able to get away at the present time.'

'So, tell me about Richard.' He said it quite casually
but Helen thought she detected an edge to his tone that
she couldn't quite identify. She looked up sharply but
he was enthusiastically tucking into his avocado and as-
paragus.

'What do you want to know?' she asked guardedly.

'Well, you two are quite obviously an item and it
intrigues me.'

'Whatever do you mean?' Helen stared at him across
the table.

'I suppose because you came across as being so ill
suited. No, please.' He held up his hand when she
opened her mouth to protest. 'Please, don't take offence—it was merely the observation of an outsider.'

'Richard and I have known each other for a very long
time,' she retorted defensively.

'So have a lot of people, but that fact alone doesn't
automatically guarantee compatibility.'

'Well, no.' She paused. 'But that doesn't apply in our case. We are very compatible.'

'Really?' He raised his eyebrows and to her further irritation, he said, 'You amaze me.'

'I can't think why that should amaze you. You hardly know me and you've only met Richard once—not very much, you must admit, to form that sort of judgement.'

'It wasn't a judgement, Helen, honestly,' he protested, laughing now. 'Simply an observation.'

'But based on what, for goodness' sake?' she demanded as she dabbed her mouth with her napkin then pushed her plate away.

'Well.' He paused, as if considering his reply carefully and at the same time eyeing her so speculatively that she felt embarrassed. 'I would say,' he went on at last, 'that under that slightly cool exterior of yours there beats a very passionate heart.'

She stared at him, hardly able to believe what he'd just said. 'Oh, for goodness' sake,' she said at last, giving an annoyed, dismissive little gesture.

'So correct me. Tell me I'm wrong.' His eyes widened but there was still amusement lurking there in their depths. 'I would say there are many things you care passionately about—true?'

'Yes…'

'And I would also say that you take your relationships very seriously—fidelity and commitment to one partner that sort of thing. Right again?'

'Well, yes, but…'

'So, if those things don't add up to a passionate woman—'

'Mr Sawyer,' she said in a burst of exasperation, 'if you are trying to wind me up—'

'Would I do such a thing?' With his hand on his heart he gazed innocently back at her.

As the brief flare-up of tension between them dissolved, Helen was forced to laugh.

'Shall we start again?' said Nick. 'How did you and Richard meet? And I promise this time not to be judgemental.'

'I think I've known him for ever,' said Helen slowly.

'You're both Islanders?' He looked genuinely interested now.

'Yes, Richard's older than me, but his father was our family GP. Our families were friends, our fathers both members of the same sailing and golf clubs and our mothers on the same charity committees. I…I was always very fond of Richard.'

'He's a widower, isn't he?'

Helen nodded. 'Yes, he married a girl called Diana Parker—she came from another old Island family.'

'And what about Kate—where did she fit into this happy scene? Was she also from an Island family?'

'No,' Helen replied quickly. 'Kate came from Dorset. She came to the same school that Diana and I attended but as a boarder—we were day-pupils. The three of us became firm friends—we shared everything.'

'Including boyfriends?' He was smiling as he said it.

'Of course not,' she protested.

'But Richard…surely he was your boyfriend…yet he married Diana?'

Helen was silent for a moment, staring at the table-cloth, surprised at the sudden intensity of feeling that swept over her as Nick inadvertently re-opened the old wound. 'Yes,' she said at last, 'he married Diana.'

'And what about you?'

'What about me?' Quickly she looked up, briefly allowing her eyes to meet his before just as quickly looking away again.

He didn't answer immediately, waiting as the waiter served their food and poured the wine, but at last, when they were alone again, he said, 'So, was there no one else for you?'

'No one important,' she murmured, pretending to inspect the dish of vegetables prior to serving herself.

'No one matched up to Richard?' he said softly.

'I suppose not.' She felt her cheeks redden slightly. She was amazed at the accuracy of his comments. In such a brief space of time he had analysed her situation and put into words what she had been unwilling to admit to anyone—even to her herself.

'So, what happened?'

'What do you mean—what happened?' She was on the defensive again, imagining he was probing into her own not very exciting private life.

'To Diana,' he said.

'Oh, to Diana.' She paused. 'It was terribly sad,' she said at last. 'She developed leukaemia and unfortunately didn't respond to treatment. She died about three years ago. Everyone was devastated.'

'Including Richard presumably?'

'Oh, especially Richard. I feared for his sanity at one point. I think if it hadn't been for his children he might have given up. He has two children, Alex, who is fourteen, and Cassie, who is twelve.'

'How did you and Richard get together again?' He sounded genuinely interested now, as if he really wanted to know.

Helen found herself hesitating before replying, afraid anything she might say would be misconstrued. 'It just sort of happened,' she said at last with a little shrug. 'I suppose you could say we just drifted into it. As I told you, we'd always been friends and, well, working so close together, with Richard at the Centre and me at the Shalbrooke, it was pretty inevitable that our paths would cross frequently.'

'So you've helped him to rebuild his life?'

'I hope so. I've always tried to listen whenever he wanted to talk about Diana...'

'Does that happen frequently?'

'Oh, yes, all the time.' She paused. 'He adored her, you see, and I understand that. He knows I understand so he feels able to unburden himself to me.'

'Where does all this leave you?'

'What do you mean?' She frowned.

'Well, from where I'm sitting it sounds very one-sided.'

'Oh, it isn't,' said Helen quickly. 'It isn't like that at all.'

'Well, I hope it isn't. For your sake.' He leaned forward slightly, his hazel eyes slightly troubled. 'Living in the shadow of a dead woman would be pretty demoralising for anyone, but for a passionate woman like you—'

'You're at it again!' She stared at him in exasperation.

'Sorry.' He grinned. Growing serious again, he said, 'Do you think he'll ever get over her? His late wife, I mean.'

'Well...'

'Presumably you hope so, otherwise your future would be looking pretty grim, wouldn't it?'

She took a deep breath. 'Nick, do you think we could change the subject?'

'But of course.' He leaned back in his chair and lifted his hands, the gesture submissive. 'I was just about to say the same thing. All this talk of Richard was really getting very boring. I'm sure we have much more exciting things to talk about.'

'No doubt you have some suggestions,' she said drily.

'I was going to say, let's talk about you,' he replied, and filled her wineglass.

'Well, that really would bore you.'

'On the contrary.' He leaned across the table towards her again, and with mischief in his eyes he said, 'I have the feeling that finding out everything there is to know about *you* could be very exciting indeed.'

Later, much later, he escorted her to her room, ignoring her protests that she was perfectly capable of finding her own way to the lift and then to the fourth floor. In the corridor outside her room he took her hand, kissed it and thanked her for her company.

'I'll meet you in the foyer for our walk at seven in the morning,' he said, without releasing her hand.

'I don't know about that, Nick,' she said. 'Really, I don't.'

'You don't like walking?' he asked.

'Oh, it isn't that. I love walking. I have a red setter at home who is never satisfied by however much exercise I give him...'

'Can't have you getting out of practice, then.'

'That's hardly likely in a week... I had been hoping for a bit of a rest.'

'See you in the morning.' He grinned, winked at her and, releasing her hand, said, 'Goodnight, Helen.' Then he turned and walked away from her down the long hotel corridor.

'Goodnight...Nick.' She watched his retreating figure for a moment before, with a little sigh, she let herself

into her room. Closing the door behind her, she leaned
against it for a moment and reflected on the evening.

In spite of her initial reservations at finding him there,
she was forced to admit she really had enjoyed the evening. He was such good company that she doubted anyone could be bored in his presence. She was still amazed
at the coincidence of him being there, but underneath all
that there was something else—an awareness between
them which her common sense told her she should be
wary of. It was an awareness tinged with excitement, a
dangerous awareness with strong sexual undertones that,
to Helen, was almost alien.

Her relationship with Richard was quiet, safe, with no
emotional fireworks and she knew Nick had been quick
to pick up on that, almost to question its predictability.
But it was what she wanted. What she had always
wanted and now, when it was almost within her grasp,
Nick Sawyer had come along and forced her to examine
it, to question it, even if only for a second.

With another sigh she moved away from the door and
pulled free the long chiffon scarf she wore, untying the
velvet bow and shaking loose her hair. She shouldn't go
on the walk with him in the morning, innocent as it
might appear, she knew that—knew it could easily be
misconstrued as offering him encouragement. The last
thing Mr Nick Sawyer needed was encouragement in
any shape or form.

No, she quite definitely wouldn't be going on any
early-morning strolls through the park with him. And the
more she thought about it the more she came to the
conclusion that she should make certain she wasn't ex-
clusively in his company for the duration of the conference.

Tomorrow, she thought as a little later she slipped

between the sheets, she would endeavour to meet some of the other delegates, hopefully strike up some friendships.

She was about to settle down for the night when the phone by her bedside suddenly rang.

'Just checking that you are all right.' There was no mistaking the familiar voice at the other end of the line.

'Of course I'm all right. Why shouldn't I be?'

'Well, you can't be too sure these days. Women alone in strange hotels and all that.'

'Are you trying to make me nervous?'

'Of course not. But if by any chance you should be— I'm in Room 507. If you should be feeling lonely, don't hesitate to pick up the phone. I don't care what time it is...if you need me I'll be there. I timed it and it only takes three minutes thirty seconds from your room to mine—'

'Goodnight, Nick,' she said firmly.

'Don't forget our date in the morning—'

'I said goodnight.' Firmly she replaced the phone and stared at the receiver with a mixture of amusement and exasperation. Anyone else acting in this way would have irritated her beyond measure. In fact, if it had been anyone else by now she would have probably reported them to the hotel management for harassment.

But somehow, because it was Nick, it was different. Nick was a friend of Jon Hammond, but it wasn't just that... There was something more to it than that...

The phone rang again. With another sigh she lifted the receiver. 'I told you—goodnight,' she said.

'Helen? Helen, is that you?'

She sat bolt upright in bed. 'Oh, Richard,' she said. 'It's you.'

'Yes,' he replied. 'It's me. Who did you think it was?'

'Oh, no one. It doesn't matter. I wasn't expecting you to phone, that's all. It's lovely to hear your voice.'

He laughed. 'You sound as if we haven't seen each other for weeks. It was only this morning that I took you to the ferry.'

'Yes, I know. It seems ages ago somehow. And you suddenly seem very far away.'

'You're only in London, Helen—it's hardly the other side of the world.'

'I know, Richard. I know.'

'So, how's it going? Hotel all right?'

'Yes, it's very nice. I have a room overlooking the park.'

'Early morning walks, then?'

'Er...yes, possibly.'

'What about the sessions—anything interesting yet?'

'Not really—hasn't really got going yet—but the itinerary sounds very promising.'

'What about the other delegates? Anyone there that we know?'

She swallowed. 'Actually, yes, you'll be amazed—I certainly was—but Nick Sawyer is here. You remember Nick?'

'Can't say that I do.'

'He was Jon Hammond's best man.' Even to herself her voice sounded strange, more high-pitched than usual. Goodness knows how it must have sounded to Richard.

'Oh yes, I remember him.' Richard hadn't seemed to notice anything amiss. 'First-rate fellow. And you say he's there at the conference?'

'Yes...'

'Well, I'm glad. It makes so much difference if there's a familiar face at these things—I know, I've been on enough of them in my time. Anyway, remember me to him, won't you?'

'Yes, Richard, I will.'

'Well, I'd best be off now. Get some sleep. Take care of yourself.'

'I will. Thanks for phoning, Richard. I'll give you a call later in the week.'

After they had said goodnight Helen replaced the receiver and for the second time that night found herself staring at it, her mind in sudden, inexplicable turmoil.

CHAPTER THREE

'YOU weren't there,' Nick whispered as he slipped into the seat beside Helen in the conference hall.

'I overslept,' she murmured out of the corner of her mouth. The chairman had already begun his opening remarks and a hush was rapidly descending on the delegates.

'You missed a treat,' he murmured in reply, and when she gave a little shrug he added, 'Never mind, there's always tomorrow.'

She chose to ignore that, attempting instead to concentrate on what was being said on the platform, mindful that Richard would be sure to want an in-depth account of the proceedings.

It had been Richard's phone call the previous night that had rapidly brought her to her senses and banished any notions she may have been harbouring of early morning strolls through the park with dangerously attractive fellow delegates.

The theme for that day's lectures and discussions was alternative medicine of Oriental origin. Helen quickly became absorbed in a highly fascinating talk from a Chinese delegate on his culture's practices and theories and its approach to healing.

'How d'you think that would go down on a busy morning on A and E?' whispered Nick in her ear as, amidst a round of enthusiastic applause, the lecture came to a close.

'Probably with a fair degree of suspicion from the "give me something now" brigade,' Helen admitted.

'Just what I was thinking,' Nick agreed. 'I always think these things sound wonderful at the time—but try putting them into practice and I fear it could be another matter. Imagine someone brought into Cas in agony and telling them to hold on while you try out one of those procedures just to see if it has any effect. All most people want, in my experience, is a swift shot of pethidine to get them out of pain.'

'I think these sorts of ideas are more appropriate to general practice than to our line of business,' Helen replied.

'I agree,' said Nick with a nod. 'The next lecture is probably more of the same so how about you and I play hooky and slope off somewhere?'

'Absolutely not,' said Helen firmly.

'Oh, well, it was worth a try,' sighed Nick. 'But I'll settle for coffee instead—come on, we've got half an hour's break.' He stood up, not giving her a chance to refuse, and made his way to the rear of the hall.

While she was waiting for him to fetch their coffee a fellow delegate came up to her, smiled and nodded. 'Hello,' she said, 'I'm Anne Longman from Salisbury. I'm a pharmacist.'

'Hello.' Helen smiled back. 'Helen Turner from the Isle of Wight. I'm a nursing sister in Accident and Emergency.'

'And what about your husband?' The woman turned to look at Nick who was on his way back with two cups of coffee.

'Oh, he isn't my husband,' said Helen quickly.

'Really?' The woman looked up swiftly. 'I imagined he was.'

'Actually, we hardly know each other…' Helen trailed off, suddenly aware how that must sound to anyone who had observed herself and Nick last night in the bar, then at their cosy table for two in the hotel dining room and again this morning seated together in the conference hall.

As Nick came up to them and passed Helen her coffee she couldn't fail to notice the appreciation in Anne Longman's eyes as the other woman allowed her gaze to roam over the handsome doctor.

'Hello,' he said, and in the brief pause that followed Helen realised Anne was waiting for an introduction.

'Oh, Nick,' she said, 'this is Anne Longman from Salisbury. Anne is a pharmacist. Anne, this is Nick Sawyer from Norfolk. Nick is working in A and E at the moment but has until recently been working for the VSO.'

'I say, how exciting,' said Anne, her voice suddenly low and slightly husky as she took Nick's hand. 'What part of the world were you in?'

'Most recently in the mountains and hill country around Nepal.'

'Oh, how wonderful.' She sighed, rolling her large expressive eyes dramatically. 'You've been to Katmandu?'

Nick nodded.

'That's the one place on earth I've always wanted to visit. It sounds so romantic. You must tell me about it.'

After Nick had secured a further cup of coffee for Anne the three of them sat together and for the entire half-hour break Anne proceeded to commandeer Nick's attention, but instead of listening to him she spent the time talking non-stop about herself.

When the bell sounded to indicate a return to the conference hall Helen found herself feeling vaguely disappointed that the break was over and she and Nick had said virtually nothing to each other.

The second session of the day concerned antibiotics—their effectiveness, the result of their overuse and the disturbing reports of growing incidences of immunity. Helen became deeply engrossed as these were topics that directly involved her own work.

Immediately after the lecture she found herself drawn into discussion with a group of delegates who were sitting directly behind herself and Nick. Two of them were nurses and when they discovered that Helen was also a nurse the conversation deepened, switching from hospital trusts to management procedures and budgeting controls.

When eventually she stood up and looked around there was no sign of Nick and she assumed he had already left the hall.

On entering the bar with her newly acquired acquaintances, Helen saw him at a table with Anne Longman in what appeared to be deep conversation, with Anne gazing adoringly up into his face.

That didn't take him long, she thought. He was quite obviously the type of man who lapped up female attention. Well, maybe it wasn't a bad thing because it would give her a rest from his attentions and perhaps at the same time give her the chance to meet a few more people.

She quickly found herself drawn into the group of people with whom she'd been talking. Someone bought her a drink and someone else asked her to join them for lunch, and when, out of the corner of her eye, she saw Nick trying to catch her attention she took a secret little delight in pretending she hadn't noticed him.

She saw him again later in the dining room, still in

the company of Anne Longman, at a table in the window, while she sat with the others and joined in their banter and light-hearted conversation. The food was good and the company pleasant so at the end of what should have been an enjoyable hour Helen was quite at a loss to explain why she felt slightly depressed.

The afternoon session had been divided into groups and Helen found herself in the hotel's Green Drawing Room in the company of other nursing staff. She hadn't seen in which direction Nick had gone, but no doubt his new companion had somehow made sure she was in the same group as him even if the organisers hadn't put doctors and pharmacists together.

By the time she returned to her room at the end of the day's lectures Helen had developed a headache, and on the spur of the moment decided to have dinner brought to her room, instead of facing the fray in the dining room. The thought of sharing a table with Nick Sawyer and Anne Longman was somehow more than she could cope with. Neither did a riotous meal with her new friends appeal while Nick and Anne sat in a secluded tête-à-tête in another part of the same room.

She half expected him to phone and demand to know why she wasn't coming down, and then later, after she'd eaten, to find out what was wrong—why she hadn't appeared. But the phone remained ominously quiet for the entire evening and by the time Helen got into bed her headache, if anything, was worse, and she felt more depressed than ever.

To make matters worse she dreamt about Nick Sawyer that night. Strange dreams where he was chasing her through a park. But it wasn't one of the beautiful London parks in its autumn glory, it was a park of dark trees with gnarled trunks and branches like tentacles that trailed and clung to her fleeing form. And when, at last, he caught her, he wasn't alone. Anne Longman was there also and she watched while Nick made love to Helen, laughing hideously as she tried to protest, to fight him off.

Then the dream changed and they were no longer in the dark wood but in a sweet-smelling meadow full of buttercups, she and Nick. They were alone this time and his love-making was gentle and tender and so sweet that she cried out with love for him, only to find when she opened her eyes that he had turned into Richard.

She awoke with a start and lay with her heart thumping, staring at the ceiling, as gradually her brain accepted the fact that it had only been a dream.

It had seemed so real. She had felt his touch, the feel of his skin bare against her own, his warm breath, the taste of him as his mouth had covered hers. Then his hand on her breast, teasing and arousing her, and the hardening of his body followed by the swift shaft of desire as he had entered her. It had been then, during the exciting rhythm of his love-making and only seconds away from the promised explosion that would tip them both into the promised abyss, that she had opened her eyes.

And now, because it had all been so real, as she thought of Richard she felt a wave of guilt rush over her, which was crazy when she considered that nothing had happened and that there was nothing for her to feel remotely guilty about.

Why, she hadn't even had dinner with Nick the previous evening. He, no doubt, had enjoyed the company of Anne Longman who had made very plain her interest in him. They had probably even extended the evening. A stroll in the park, perhaps? Dancing in the hotel bar, followed by a nightcap and then...what then? Had he escorted Anne to her room just as he had herself the night before, and whereas she had bade him a firm goodnight and sent him on his way had Anne perhaps invited him in? Had he stayed?

She glanced at the bedroom clock and saw that it was two-thirty. Were they even now in bed? Was Nick caressing Anne, making love to her just as he had to Helen in that meadow amongst the buttercups? A stab of pain suspiciously akin to jealousy shot through her.

But this was ridiculous, she told herself sharply. He hadn't made love to her. That had been a dream, albeit a very real one. And, besides, what should it matter to her if he was in Anne Longman's bed at two-thirty in the morning? It was of no concern of hers what he did. Neither did she care... Even if he'd made love to the wretched woman half a dozen times she didn't care...

And, if that was the case, she hoped the pair of them would look absolutely shattered and thoroughly haggard the following morning at breakfast so that the other delegates would all know what they had been up to.

Turning over, she determinedly thumped her pillow. She would forget Nick Sawyer, Anne Longman and even Richard, and go back to sleep.

Sleep, however, proved to be an elusive bedfellow and by the end of a night of tossing and turning Helen feared it would be she who would appear shattered and haggard at the breakfast table.

It was well before seven o'clock when she slipped out of the hotel entrance. The only people who were around were the hotel doorman, who bade her a cheery good morning, the postman and a couple of delivery men who were reversing their van into the road alongside the hotel.

The pale, early morning sunshine was struggling through the mist while the iron railings surrounding the park were festooned with spiders' webs, sparkling with dew. There was little traffic about and, after crossing the road, Helen began to walk the paths between avenues of trees already glowing in their autumnal colours as the sun gently touched and awoke them.

She was still some distance from a figure sitting on the park bench when she realised with a little jolt that it was Nick. As she approached he didn't look up, but merely moved along to make room for her.

'You know,' he said as she sat down beside him, 'I still have a difficulty fathoming a woman's reasoning.'

'Now why would that be?' Throwing him a sidelong glance, she saw that this morning he was casually dressed in cords and a thick navy sweater.

'Well, yesterday morning when I was so sure you would join me there was no sign of you, but this morning when I wouldn't have given my chances a hope in hell—here you are.'

'I didn't know you would be here,' she said. 'I simply felt in need of fresh air and exercise.'

'So are you saying you wouldn't have come if you'd known?' The glance he gave her was cool, with none of his previous humour or the slightly outrageous manner that she had come to associate with him. Quite suddenly, irrationally, she regretted the absence of both.

'Not really,' she said. She paused. 'I guess if I'd thought about it I might have assumed you would be otherwise engaged this morning.'

He frowned. 'What do you mean?'

'I probably would have thought that, had you been

coming to the park, you would have been accompanied by Ms Longman,' she replied lightly.

For one moment he looked totally blank and Helen found herself thinking that she might have misjudged him. 'I thought,' she went on swiftly, giving him no chance to speak, 'that she seemed to have attached herself to you pretty firmly yesterday.'

'Not so firmly that I wasn't able to do a speedy extrication,' he said crisply, and added, 'If there's one thing I can't cope with it's a predatory female. Anyway...' he paused fractionally '...I think she's now got the message. Last night at dinner she had attached herself to some other poor fellow—a young junior houseman, I believe. No doubt we'll find her consuming him at breakfast along with her cornflakes.'

So she had been wrong. Quite wrong, she thought as they sat in silence and watched a squirrel as it darted back and forth across the grass. All that she had imagined had been happening between Nick Sawyer and Anne Longman had been simply that—a figment of her imagination.

But now just thinking of it revived other thoughts, those of the dream she'd had, thoughts which hadn't been too far from her mind ever since, exhausted, she'd finally got out of her bed.

'Actually,' he said at last, breaking the silence between them, 'it made me think.'

'What did?' She threw him another glance.

'How much she irritated me,' he said. 'And I found myself wondering,' he went on, 'if I had irritated you.'

'Why should you think that?'

'Well, I suppose I might have come on rather strong. And, well, you did appear to be trying to avoid me, and later when you didn't show for dinner... Anyway, if that was the case, I'm sorry, Helen.'

'It's OK,' she replied, touched by his apparent sincerity. 'Really it is. The only reason I didn't come down to dinner last night was because I had a headache. I had a tray sent up to my room.'

He looked up quickly and as she saw the eagerness in his eyes it dawned on her that they had both been the victims of misapprehension. In that moment she was aware of being pleased, quite inordinately so, that he hadn't slept with Anne Longman.

'Perhaps we should start again,' he said with a sudden, almost boyish grin. 'I won't harass you again, I promise...'

'And I won't abandon you to the tender mercies of predatory females.'

They both laughed and the squirrel, startled by the sudden noise, scampered away and darted up the trunk of a tall conifer.

'I guess,' Helen said after a moment, 'I guess maybe I should apologise as well. I didn't mean to put you down quite so strongly as I did. It's just that—'

'I know,' he sighed. 'You and Richard are an item, and you don't want any complications. Is that it?'

'Something like that.' She nodded.

He was silent for a moment then asked thoughtfully, 'After Kate's and Jon's wedding, when you caught Kate's bouquet, there was plenty of speculation that you would be the next one in the marriage stakes. How accurate were those forecasts?'

'Probably pretty accurate...' She shrugged.

'Have you set a date?'

'Heavens, no,' she said quickly. 'It's just become an

unspoken agreement between us that one day we'll be together.'

'You mean married, or living together?' He threw her a curious but strangely concerned glance.

Again she shrugged.

'I would have thought marriage would be essential to you, as opposed to cohabiting,' he went on after a moment.

'Well, yes, I suppose it is.' She hesitated. 'In our case, Richard's and mine, though, it hasn't all been exactly straightforward. You see, after Diana's death my father's illness grew worse and practically all my time was taken up, caring for him. During that time poor Richard barely got a look-in. He's been very patient. A lot of men simply wouldn't have been prepared to put up with a situation like that.'

'Your father died during the summer, didn't he?' asked Nick after a moment, and when Helen nodded in agreement he said, 'But Richard hasn't pressed you to set a date since then or to make plans?'

'No, not really.' She shook her head and then, fearing he might have misinterpreted the situation, said, 'There's no hurry, Nick, really there isn't. Richard's giving me time, that's all.' She glanced quickly at him as she spoke and to her consternation found he was watching her closely.

'I'm not sure I'd be able to do the same,' he said quietly.

'What do you mean?' She frowned, wondering what on earth he was going to say.

'If it were me, I wouldn't be able to wait,' he said. 'I would want you too much. I'd want to make you mine—'

'I...' Covered in sudden confusion, she lifted her

hand, the gesture both dismissive and restraining, but, undaunted, Nick carried on.

'Just in case some arrogant, conceited bastard came along and swept you away from me. You know the type I mean—the sort of guy you meet at one of those medical conferences.'

She laughed, amused once more by his audacity. 'Nick Sawyer,' she said severely, 'you are utterly incorrigible, you know. Here was I only a few moments ago thinking you had turned over a new leaf, and now here you are being as outrageous as ever.'

He shrugged. 'Well, at least we know where we stand now,' he said lightly.

'Do we?'

'Yes.' He nodded. 'You have Richard to whom you will return at the end of the week. I know that and fully understand it so I'll make no demands on you that you feel unable to fulfil.'

He stood up and for a moment he stared down at her with his head tilted thoughtfully to one side, as if considering the situation. He looked serious and Helen wondered what he was thinking. Then his eyes crinkled at the corners in that very attractive way that she had come to associate with him and he held out his hand.

'Come on,' he said, 'let's go back to the hotel and have breakfast together.'

Raising her hand, she allowed him to grasp it to assist her to her feet, but as they began to walk, and when he failed to release it, she tugged to free herself.

Nick, however, seemed oblivious to her intention and, still holding her hand, tucked her arm through his. 'Let's enjoy this glorious morning,' he said. 'Look, the mist has nearly gone, the sunshine is winning, the leaves have barely begun to fall and I'm in the company of the loveliest lady I know. We'll just enjoy this moment. After that, I promise I'll behave myself.'

He leaned towards her and gently brushed her cheek with his lips, then set off through the park at a cracking pace, forcing her almost to run to keep up with him but leaving her no other option as he still held tightly on to her hand.

The lectures that day and the ensuing discussions concerned the importance of the identification of the source of a patient's problem instead of the automatic and often unnecessary treatment of a whole variety of symptoms.

Helen took copious notes, knowing that these topics could well interest Richard or even Kate and Jon, and by the end of the day her head was spinning with all the facts, figures, theories and statistics.

'I think it would do us good to get away from this place for a while.' Nick yawned and stretched as the final session of the day came to a close.

'I think you could be right.' Helen nodded wearily. Glancing at her watch, she said, 'What did you have in mind? We've got a couple of hours before dinner.'

'I was going to suggest we skip dinner—at least here at the hotel, that is. I know a nice little restaurant just off Covent Garden. I'll give them a ring and see if I can reserve a table. What do you say?'

She hesitated as alarm bells began to go off warningly in her head.

'Promise I'll behave,' he said, with one hand on his heart.

'Then how can I refuse?' she said helplessly. After all, what harm could come from dinner whether it was here in the hotel or somewhere else? 'I'll go and change,' she added as they both stood.

On the way out of the conference hall they saw Anne Longman with her junior doctor in attendance. She pointedly ignored them both.

'Glad to see he's still in one piece,' murmured Nick with a wicked chuckle.

In her room Helen took a long leisurely bath, relaxing in the scented water, while she deliberated on what she could wear from the very limited wardrobe she had brought with her.

She hoped she wouldn't regret her decision to go to dinner with Nick. It would certainly make a nice change from the hotel dining room, pleasant as that was, and he had, after all, promised to behave himself. He knew the score now regarding herself and Richard so she doubted that she would have any bother with him, and when all was said and done he really was very nice.

She leaned back against the rim of the bath and closed her eyes. Idly she allowed herself to speculate what it might be like if she didn't have Richard, and found herself admitting that, yes, in those circumstances she really did feel she could have gone for Nick Sawyer in a big way. It wasn't just his looks, devastating as they were, it was the way he smiled, his eyes crinkling at the corners, his sense of humour, which already she had found uncannily like her own, and, yes, she had to confess, the look in his eyes when on several occasions she had looked up to find him watching her.

And, she thought, shifting slightly so that the water lapped gently over her breasts, there had been that dream. Disturbing as that had been in part, it had also been exciting. Dangerously exciting, and erotic—so much so that even now, just thinking about it, she felt a slow throbbing sensation somewhere deep inside.

She hadn't felt this way for a long time. Not since…

Frowning, she tried to cast her mind back. Not really since the time she had loved Richard before…before he had married Diana. She certainly didn't feel that way now, but surely that was because she had matured since then. Either that, or it was a case of familiarity breeding contempt, she thought with a wry little smile.

Nick had questioned her relationship with Richard, questioned its direction. She hadn't really given it too much thought recently, had just assumed they would drift gently either into marriage or a state of cohabitation. Nick's questions had disturbed her. She wasn't sure why exactly, but they had. It was almost as if he had been suggesting that the relationship had gone off the boil or, even worse, had grown stale.

But that was ridiculous. She had loved Richard for as long as she could remember. When he had married Diana, preferring her friend to herself, Helen had been devastated, but she had carefully concealed her hurt and had put on a brave face to their mutual friends and to the world. But there had never really been anyone else, at least, not seriously. Richard had been the only one.

After Diana's death she had been there for him, and had helped him pick up the pieces and put his life back together. Then had come her father's illness and everyone had come to assume that it was only that which had stopped them from getting together.

But now Harry was gone, and they were no nearer naming the day.

Maybe Nick was right.

Restlessly she moved again and realised that the water was growing cold. With a sigh she sat up, let the water go and stood, reaching for a large fluffy towel and wrapping herself comfortingly in its folds.

She wouldn't think about it now. Tonight she would enjoy herself. She would go out with Nick, there would be no strings attached and she would have fun.

CHAPTER FOUR

NICK was waiting for Helen in the foyer. Tonight he wore a cream polo-necked shirt with his dark suit. He allowed his gaze to wander over her and Helen felt ridiculously pleased that she had taken such care. She had finally decided on the black dress and had chosen to wear her blonde hair loose in a sleek bob instead of tied back as she so often did.

'You look lovely,' he said simply.

Outside the hotel Nick hailed a cab which took them to the hustle and bustle of Covent Garden. Their restaurant was in a basement, tucked away down a little side street, somewhere that would remain undiscovered unless you knew of its whereabouts. Their table was in an alcove, intimate yet from where they could observe, and absorb, the ambience.

In one corner a man in a silk brocade waistcoat played soft melodies on a piano and all around them the walls were covered with theatre posters of old shows and musicals.

The choice of menu was wide, and they took a long time to order. When at last they'd done so, Helen having chosen swordfish and Nick venison, the waiter whisked away the menus and left them to relax over aperitifs.

'Glad you came?' asked Nick, looking up and catching her gazing around.

'Yes.' She smiled. 'It's the most amazing place.'

'I thought you might like it.'

'You've obviously been here before.' She raised one eyebrow.

He nodded. 'Yes. I have.'

'What was her name?'

He smiled. 'It wasn't anything like that. No, really,' he said, catching sight of her expression. 'I was at St Thomas's hospital for a while. One of our crowd had a sister who was with the Royal Shakespeare Company. She brought us here once after a performance and after that it became a firm favourite. As you can see, it's very popular—we were lucky to get a table.'

'So it doesn't have any romantic connotations for you?' she said watching him closely.

'No, nothing like that.'

'So, are you telling me there isn't anyone?' Suddenly she was curious.

'Would that be so hard to accept?' The amusement was there again in his hazel eyes.

'Yes,' she said, setting her glass down. 'Actually, it would. I would find it very hard to accept that there isn't anyone in your life.'

'Well, that's the way it is.' He shrugged and then, with a wicked grin, he said, 'That's not to say there hasn't been, of course.'

'Oh, of course,' said Helen solemnly. 'But just not at the moment.'

'That's right.' He leaned back, as if reflecting. 'My lifestyle in recent years hasn't really lent itself to serious relationships. To put it mildly, I haven't exactly been around. Most of my time has been spent either in some remote mountain village or in a desert war zone. There really aren't too many women who are prepared to put up with that sort of thing, you know.'

'Probably not,' Helen agreed. Thoughtfully, she

added, 'But has there ever been anyone who made you consider giving up that way of life?'

'Like Kate with Jon, you mean?' He threw her a quick look and when she nodded he slowly shook his head. 'Not really,' he said, but after a slight hesitation he went on, 'There was someone once…a very long time ago now. I think I might have been able to come home and settle down with her…'

'What happened?' Helen asked gently when it seemed as if he wasn't going to volunteer any more information.

He shrugged. 'I left it too long, I guess. When I did eventually decide, I came home to find that she had met someone else. She married him and they have a couple of kids now.' He said it casually but Helen instinctively knew he had been deeply hurt.

'And nothing like that has happened since?' she said at last.

'Not like that, no… At least…' He paused and looked at her. She saw and recognized the look that came into his eyes and spoke again hurriedly to prevent him saying what she knew he'd been about to say.

'I would have liked children,' she said quickly. 'I suppose, really, that's my biggest regret, not having had any children of my own.'

He stared at her. 'There's time, for heaven's sake,' he said. 'Plenty of time.'

'Richard doesn't want more children,' she said quietly. 'He…he's been quite honest with me about that.'

'Even if you do?' His eyes met hers across the table and she was forced to look away quickly. To her relief the waiter arrived at that moment with their food and she was saved from further discussion on that particular subject.

Their conversation changed after that. They talked of

their childhoods and almost without realising it, filled in details of their lives and backgrounds and added pieces to the picture to build a whole. Helen learnt of Nick's happy childhood at his family home in Norfolk where he had grown up the youngest of a family of four, having two sisters and one brother. He in turn heard about her upbringing with her sister at the family home in Gatcombe and the trauma her family had gone through, following the death of her mother from cancer.

'It turns your life upside down, doesn't it?' he said sympathetically. 'I know it did for us when my father died.'

'What about your mother—is she still alive?' asked Helen. Suddenly she wanted to know. She wanted to know everything there was to know about him.

'Yes, she still lives at the family home. It's too big for her, really, but she doesn't want to move. She has so many memories there of my father, and there's her garden. She couldn't bear to lose her garden. My sisters and my brother live nearby and they all help.'

'And what about you?' said Helen mischievously. 'Do you help as well?'

'As much as I can. Yes.' He nodded. 'When I'm here, that is. But I think I'm the bane of her life.'

'Oh, and why is that?'

'She despairs of me. I'm the only one who isn't married. All she wants is for me to settle down, marry and give her yet more grandchildren to add to the brood she already has. Oh, and to go into the practice, of course.'

'The practice?' she said quickly.

'Yes, the one my father founded.'

'Your father was a GP?' she said, and when he nodded she added, 'I hadn't realised that.'

'Oh, yes, and the big plan was always for me to follow

in his footsteps.' Nick pulled a face. 'I, of course, re-
belled and rejected the whole thing,' he went on after a
moment, 'and, after qualifying, I took myself off to foreign parts. The more foreign and the more far-flung the
better—anything rather than do what was expected of
me.'

'So, what about your brother?' Helen was really curious now. 'Is he a doctor? Couldn't he fulfil the family
destiny?'

'No.' Nick shook his head. 'Marcus is a barrister. He
was clever, and had the ability to look ahead at a very
early age. I allowed myself to be channelled, then re-
sented it.'

'Isn't rebellion a strange thing?' said Helen slowly.
'We so often spend half a lifetime engaged in it, then
the other half settling for what we had so actively re-
belled against.'

'Are you saying I should marry, have a family and
settle for the life of a country GP?' asked Nick thoughtfully.

'I don't know.' Helen shrugged. 'But, presumably,
you can't keep climbing mountains for ever. I guess
there comes a time when we all have to take stock of
what we have and of what choices are available to us.
And, from what you have described, it doesn't sound as
if that option would be so terrible—a ready established
rural practice. There are a lot of people I know who
would probably give their eye teeth for such an opportunity.'

'Maybe,' he said, 'but I think you may be forgetting
something.'

'Oh, and what's that?' she asked innocently knowing
full well what his answer would be.

'To complete that rosy picture,' he said, 'I would need the right woman.'

'Ah, that woman you once told me you haven't yet met?' she said softly.

'Did I say that?' He raised his eyebrows. 'Maybe when I said it I believed it. Maybe now it would be different.'

She knew what he meant, knew from every look, every gesture, he gave what he meant, and somehow, for the moment at least, she seemed powerless to stop it.

As the evening went on she doubted whether she wanted to stop it. They finished their meal, lingered over coffee and discussed their likes and dislikes in films, books and music, which proved to be remarkably similar. Later, much later, when there were very few people left in the place Nick drew her to her feet and onto the tiny space that served as a dance floor, and while the man in the corner continued to coax old melodies, bittersweet with nostalgia, from the keys he held her close.

For the moment she was content to let it be—to feel the beating of his heart close to her own, the touch of his hands, firm yet tender, and the feel of his cheek slightly rough against the smoothness of her own. It was a very long time since she'd been held by a man other than Richard. It felt exciting and dangerous, two emotions that were unfamiliar to Helen—so unfamiliar she wondered if she would experience either ever again.

'Helen...?' he said once, but she lifted her hand lightly and pressed her fingers against his lips, preventing him from saying what she feared he might have been about to say.

For the moment she didn't want to think, to contemplate the possible consequences of their actions or where they might lead. She didn't want to think about the future or the past, about Richard or about the girl who had broken Nick's heart all those years ago. She wanted the world to go away.

And even later in the cab when Nick took her in his arms and kissed her she was still prepared to throw caution to the winds, to live for the moment and enjoy the feel of his mouth over hers.

Only on their return to the hotel, where they were greeted by a group of fellow delegates who were gathered in the foyer, did any sense of propriety return. She was able to send Nick away to his own room, albeit with a pang of regret.

That day was to become the pattern for the remaining days of the conference—an early morning walk in the park, a shared breakfast, seated together for lectures, lunch taken in the hotel's garden room, and dinner, either at the hotel where a table for two became the norm or out to another restaurant, returning late.

The topics of the lectures began to merge in Helen's head, their details becoming hopelessly blurred. She struggled to remain in control and continue with her notes, especially with the section on alternative medicines. Aromatherapy was a topic which had always interested her and she battled to concentrate on the lecture.

'Maybe,' Nick murmured in her ear when it was almost over, 'we should find these things easier if we put them into practice.'

'What do you mean?' she whispered.

'You could always try giving me a massage with aromatic oils…'

He was almost as impossible after the lecture on reflexology. 'I had no idea the feet played such a crucial part in diagnosis,' he said. 'I know a lot of people can hardly bear to have anyone else touch their feet but I have to say I quite enjoy it. It would make a difference who was doing it, of course…'

When it came to the lecture on homeopathy—or the study of medicine based on the principle that a substance which can produce symptoms in a healthy person can help cure those symptoms in a sick person by stimulating the body's natural healing responses—Helen, in a last desperate attempt to concentrate, refused to sit beside Nick.

In the normal course of events she would have found all these topics deeply interesting but now, she was at last forced to admit, they all paled into insignificance. The only thing that mattered now was Nick Sawyer, and being able to spend as much time as possible with him before the sands of time ran out.

They talked at every possible moment, continuing to fill in every conceivable detail of each other's backgrounds so that as the week drew to a close they both admitted they felt as if they had known each other for a lifetime.

On their last evening, almost by some unspoken agreement, Nick booked a table at the Covent Garden restaurant.

By some magical coincidence they were shown to the same table by the same waiter, and in the corner the same man played the piano.

'I think they must have put it all on hold just for us,' said Helen, as their glances met and held above the rims of their wineglasses.

'I'd have been mortified if it had been any different,' Nick admitted with a laugh. 'I guess we're just a pair of incurable romantics.'

Helen sighed. 'Yes,' she agreed, 'I dare say you're

right. I suppose you could say I've always been a sucker for romance. So much so, in fact,' she added after a moment's reflection, 'that it's got me something of a reputation at home.'

'Sounds intriguing.' Nick's eyes widened. 'Tell me about it.'

'Well,' she paused again, 'I seem to have inadvertently been responsible for bringing couples together.' Smiling, she began to pleat the edge of her napkin.

'Including Kate and Jon?' he asked, and she could tell by the way he said it that his curiosity was really aroused now.

'In a way.' She nodded. 'There was a bit of misunderstanding between them which, I suppose, I helped to sort out and, well, the next thing we knew they were moving in together!' She paused again. 'Then there was another couple,' she went on at last. 'Georgina Merrick—'

'The staff nurse on your unit?' Nick interrupted.

'Yes.' She nodded. 'And her husband, Andrew…'

'Don't tell me you were responsible for their marriage as well?' His eyes were brimming with humour now.

'Maybe not originally,' Helen replied, 'but I think I may have lent a hand the second time around. They'd divorced, you see,' she added when she saw Nick's slightly bemused expression. 'Andrew was working on the unit and they were living their own lives. Georgina was at home, caring for their two daughters, but I knew she wanted to return to work. When her old job became vacant on A and E I tipped her off, she applied, I provided a reference and she came back to work. Seeing them together again I soon realised that what I had long suspected was true and that Andrew was still in love with her.'

'What about her? Was she still in love with him?'

'I don't think she'd ever really stopped loving him,' Helen replied slowly. 'But she had to learn to forgive him—he'd had an affair, you see—and to trust him again. I like to think I helped her to see things in perspective, and I also think I persuaded Andrew not to give up where Georgina and his girls were concerned.'

'My word.' Nick stared at her. 'Quite the little matchmaker, aren't you?' he said softly.

She flushed. 'I just like people to be happy,' she said.

'Well, that's two couples,' he said. 'Are there any more lurking in the background?'

'Funny you should say that.' Helen bit her lip, then laughed.

'You mean there are?' Nick stared at her.

'Yes.' She pulled a face. 'Only one,' she added hastily, 'but this one was a bit different—it sort of happened in reverse.'

'Tell me about it.' He leaned back in his chair in apparent amusement.

'I don't want to bore you,' she protested.

'You won't bore me. It's fascinating. Who was it this time—another of your nurses?'

Helen shook her head. 'No,' she said slowly, 'actually, it was a young relative of mine. My cousin's daughter. Her name's Siobhan—Siobhan O'Mara. At least, it was. She came to this country from Ireland.'

'You amaze me,' he said. 'I would never have guessed.'

'Do you want me to continue with this story or not?'

'Sorry.' He chuckled. 'Go on.'

'Well, she came here to work as a paramedic. Almost as soon as she arrived she fell for her partner, a fellow paramedic by the name of Dave Morey.'

'Don't tell me,' Nick said with a sigh. 'You introduced them?'

'No.'

'Then you encouraged their romance?'

'I most certainly did not,' Helen replied firmly. 'Dave Morey was totally unsuitable. He had a very dubious track record where women were concerned—he was the last person I thought Siobhan should get involved with. I told her so as well. But would she listen? Probably the fact that he was so unsuitable made him all the more attractive. Anyway, the next thing I knew she was head over heels in love with him.'

As she finished speaking Helen realised that Nick was laughing openly now. 'I'm glad you find this so amusing,' she said wryly. 'I was the one who had to face her mother.'

'So, what happened?'

'Oh, they are married now.' She gave a dismissive little gesture with her hands, as if the whole thing was totally beyond her control.

'And is it proving to be the disaster you predicted?' he asked softly, leaning across the table and taking her hand.

'Actually, no,' she admitted. 'I've had to eat my words where Dave Morey is concerned. I know it's early days yet, they were only married last month, but I must confess I saw another, unexpected side to Dave when my father died and, well, I have to say, he does seem to adore Siobhan...'

'And Siobhan?' said Nick gently.

'She thinks the sun shines out of him.'

'Well, there you are, then. Maybe the right woman hadn't come along before for Dave and then when he met Siobhan… It does happen, you know.' His eyes met hers again.

She stared at him for a long moment, the expression in his eyes reflecting her own thoughts. 'Yes,' she agreed at last, 'yes, I know it does.'

They danced when they had finished their meal, as they had before, but this time when Nick held her close there was a touch of desperation about the moment as they grew silent in anticipation of the following day's parting.

In the cab on their way back to the hotel the desperation was there again in his kiss. Helplessly she clung to him as wave after wave of desire swept over her, and when finally they reached the hotel and stepped out of the lift neither questioned the fact that they were on the fifth floor and not the fourth because the agreement and the understanding between them was total and utterly inevitable.

'This is the beginning and the end,' she told him, deep in the darkness.

'I know.' His reply held anguished regret but acceptance, then he reached out for her again and the certainty of their parting once more became obliterated by the piercing sweetness of their love-making.

And still Helen was prepared to live for the moment. There would be time enough tomorrow for recriminations or regret. Tonight she belonged to herself and Nick. Tonight was theirs alone, but as he brought her time and again to unfamiliar and earth-shattering fulfilment she knew that, whatever the future held, for her nothing would ever be quite the same again.

'No goodbyes, no regrets,' she wrote on the piece of hotel notepaper that she left beside the sleeping man the following morning. And to show she meant it she had packed, checked out and hailed a cab before any of her fellow delegates had so much as surfaced in the aftermath of the farewell drinks party that had been held the night before.

It wasn't until she was safely in the black cab, heading for Waterloo, that she faced the finality of her decision.

Nick would be awake by now, would have discovered that she had gone without a word, would know that now this really was the end.

It was then that she felt the tears running down her cheeks. Tears that hastily, almost angrily, she dashed away with the back of her hand.

He, too, would pack, maybe have breakfast, then take a cab to his station to catch the train that would take him back to Norfolk. Shortly he would be returning abroad to some obscure outpost, while she would return to her home, her job and Richard, and she would probably never see him again.

It was as she thought of Richard that she remembered with a little jolt that she had promised to ring him at the end of the week. She felt a stab of guilt, then wearily she leaned back against the seat and closed her eyes. The guilt at not phoning him was only a drop in the ocean compared with the enormity of what else had happened.

But she couldn't think about that yet. Time enough later when she was home. Now she was still in London. Nick was still in London. For the last few moments they were breathing the same air of the same city, something that might never happen again. She swallowed, and blinked furiously.

'Nice morning, miss.' The cabby broke into her thoughts, forcing her to concentrate on him.

'Oh, yes,' she said quickly, 'yes, it is.'

'Got far to go, have you?' He glanced at her in his driving mirror.

'Er, not really. The Isle of Wight, actually.'

'Isle of Wight, eh? The missus and I go there for our holidays. Caravan site near Shanklin—I expect you know it. It's the one with its own swimming pool. Nice spot it is. We wouldn't go anywhere else...'

Helen let him talk and he didn't seem to mind that she wasn't replying or even listening.

At Waterloo she paid the fare, picked up her case, walked into the station and joined the throng of early morning commuters.

She saw him immediately. He was standing by the paper stall, reading a copy of *The Times*. Her heart leapt, then seemed to turn right over. How he had done it she couldn't imagine, getting there before her, but miraculously he had. She started forward and wove her way through the crowd, all the time keeping him in her sights. She had almost reached him when he looked up. He turned his head and slightly surprised quizzical brown eyes met hers.

'Oh,' she muttered, overcome by sudden confusion. 'I'm sorry, I thought you were someone else.'

The pain of disappointment as she watched the man walk away was almost physical. With a sigh she turned, and as an announcement came over the address system that the train for Portsmouth Harbour was now waiting she began to walk towards platform nine.

Because Nick so dominated her thoughts she was convinced she saw him at least three more times on the journey home—once on the train, once in the crowd waiting for the ferry and, surely, that was him amongst the passengers waiting at Ryde Pier Head.

And each time she had to console herself—remind herself that it wasn't him, that it couldn't possibly be him and that even now Nick Sawyer was travelling in the opposite direction, out of her life for ever.

CHAPTER FIVE

'HELEN? Where are you?'

'I'm at home, Richard.'

'At home? But when did you get back?'

'Somewhere around lunchtime, I think it was.' She was deliberately evasive.

'You should have called me. I would have picked you up from the ferry.'

'That's all right, Richard—but thanks anyway.'

'So, how are you? How did it all go?'

'Very well.'

'Good. I can't wait to hear all about it. Shall I come over a bit later?'

'Actually, Richard, if you don't mind, I'm going to have a hot bath and an early night. I'm very tired.'

'All right. I'll see you tomorrow then.'

He would have hung up but, almost as an afterthought, she said, 'Richard, is everything all right?'

'What? Oh, yes, same as ever,' he replied. 'See you.'

A wave of depression swept over her as she replaced the receiver. Same as ever, he'd said. Same place, same job, same people—everything still the same. Only now it wasn't because everything had changed—in the space of one short week her whole world had been turned upside down and inside out—but she had to go on, to continue as if nothing had happened.

With a sigh she opened the kitchen door and stepped outside into the courtyard of her beloved garden. It was almost dusk, the scent of wood-smoke filled the air and in the distance she heard a muted bang as some over-enthusiastic person anticipated the forthcoming Guy Fawkes celebrations. Chester, newly home from the neighbour who had cared for him in her absence, padded silently behind her. When it became apparent that she didn't intend to go too far he flopped down in a heap onto the flagstones between tubs of gold and copper chrysanthemums.

The house had seemed unbearably silent on her return and she missed her father more than she had at any time since his death. Was this how it would always be now? Surely not. Surely now very soon she and Richard would marry and she would leave the Coach House and move into his house at Newtown Creek. The house where Diana had lived, the house that was still full of reminders of her—her possessions, her photographs, her books, her children. And her husband.

A shiver touched Helen's spine. Suddenly, given the choice of the two, the prospect of a solitary existence at the Coach House seemed to have the most appeal, but she knew that was not the way it would be. The unspoken agreement between herself and Richard had long been that when she was free from caring for Harry there would be nothing to stop them from being together. That time had now come. So why did the years seem to stretch away in front of her like some long, empty tunnel?

Feeling Chester's wet nose nuzzling her hand, she reached down and absent-mindedly patted the old dog's head. 'You're glad to have me back, old boy, aren't you?' she murmured. 'And I'm glad to be back. In fact, if I'm honest I'm beginning to wish I'd never gone.'

She didn't mean it, of course. She wouldn't have missed it for the world. It was just that the thought of what had happened was enough to make the rest of her life seem unimaginable if it was to be endured without Nick.

'Are you all right, Helen?' Georgina Merrick drew the curtains around the patient they had been attending and looked curiously at Helen.

'Yes, I'm fine.' Helen stiffened. 'Why?'

'I don't know…you seem…I don't know…' Georgina shrugged '…different somehow.'

'What do you mean?' Helen gave a short, forced laugh. 'Different?'

'I'm not sure. I can't explain. More…' Georgina put her head on one side, considering. 'More animated or something…'

'Oh, thanks! Are you suggesting I was dull and boring before?'

'Of course not.' Georgina laughed. 'But you do seem different ever since…ever since you came back from London. What happened up there? Did you meet some charming delegate who wined and dined you and swept you off your feet?'

'I should be so lucky!' said Helen, wondering what her friend would say if she knew just how close to the truth she was.

'Well, if I didn't know better I would say you were in love,' said Georgina.

'I am,' said Helen lightly. 'With Richard.'

'Oh, yes, yes, of course.' Georgina reddened slightly. 'How silly of me. I'd forgotten. I'm sorry, Helen, I didn't mean anything, really I didn't.'

'I know you didn't. Forget it,' Helen said, as she made her way to the treatment room. Casualties from a road traffic accident were just arriving on A and E and all hands were needed. But for once as she received the patients the procedures were automatic and her mind was elsewhere.

She had been back from London for almost a week and arguably it had been the longest week of her life as she had struggled with feelings and emotions which had swung dramatically between deep guilt at one extreme to tremendous elation and having no regrets at the other.

She had wanted to confide in someone, Kate, perhaps, or Georgina, but at the last moment something had always seemed to stop her. In the end she had come to the conclusion that it was probably better that no one else knew, not Georgina, or anyone else on A and E, or Kate, who was married to Nick's friend, Jon, and when all was said and done was Richard's partner.

'Shall I cut these trousers off?'

Helen looked up sharply as she realised that Dot Sharman was talking to her.

'What?' she said, then looked down at the patient, a middle-aged woman, and nodded. 'Oh, yes,' she said, 'yes, of course, Dot. Careful of those lacerations on her thigh. They look deep. It's all right, Mrs Naylor.' She leaned over the patient, making a supreme effort to concentrate. 'We're going to get the doctor to have a look at you.'

'My husband,' gasped the woman on the bed. 'Is he all right?'

Helen glanced at Dot who said, 'He's with the doctor now, Mrs Naylor. We're doing everything we can.'

Together they set up an intravenous infusion to replace the woman's lost fluids, checked her blood pressure and pulse rate, cut away the clothing around her injuries and staunched the blood flow.

Moments later Andrew Merrick came to examine her.

'Hello, Mrs Naylor,' he said gently. 'I'm going to take a look at these injuries.' Carefully he examined the deep lacerations on the patient's thigh. 'Looks like you had quite a disagreement with the other car,' he said. Glancing up, he added, 'X-rays, please, Sister, and cross-matching here. The orthopaedic registrar is coming down to see Mr Naylor so we can ask him to have a look at Mrs Naylor at the same time.'

'How is my husband, Doctor?' Mrs Naylor managed to lift her head.

'Not very happy,' said Andrew. 'I gather yours was a new car?'

'Oh, dear.' Mrs Naylor sank back onto the pillow. 'Yes,' she agreed, 'it was.'

'I think, Sister, we can give Mrs Naylor something to ease the pain,' said Andrew. 'Would you draw up pethidine, please?'

'Last week on the unit, Andrew,' said Helen, as she drew up the analgesic and handed him the syringe. 'How does it feel?'

'Strange,' he admitted. After he had administered the injection he said, 'I'm even beginning to think I shall miss the old place.'

'No doubt you'll be back,' said Helen, 'even if it will be in a loftier position.'

'Do we know who's taking your place yet?' asked Dot, as she drew a white cellular blanket over Mrs Naylor's legs.

'I gather Elliot has just had some details through,' said Andrew. 'Anyway, I'll leave you ladies to it. See you later, Mrs Naylor, after you've had your X-rays.'

'I shall miss him,' said Dot, as Andrew strolled in his unhurried way out of the treatment room.

'We all shall,' said Helen. 'Andrew Merrick will be

a very hard act to follow.' She turned as Dot dropped a surgical glove on the floor and, on bending to retrieve it, clutched her stomach as if in sudden pain. 'Dot?' she said sharply.

'It's all right,' said Dot.

'No, it isn't.' A quick glance at the bed confirmed that Mrs Naylor was resting comfortably so Helen ushered Dot into the sluice room. 'What's wrong?' she said.

'Don't start, please,' said Dot. 'I know what you're going to say and, yes, I've made an appointment to see my GP.'

'I'm glad to hear it,' said Helen. 'You haven't been right for some time, have you?'

'No, not really,' admitted Dot. 'My periods have been pretty horrendous and I've been getting a lot of pain each month.'

'Well, I'm pleased you're doing something about it,' said Helen, 'and not before time either. Now,' she added briskly, 'if you'll keep an eye on Mrs Naylor, I'm going to go and have a word with Elliot.'

She found the nursing manager in his office. He looked up from behind his desk as she came into the room.

'Ah, Helen,' he said, 'there you are. I was looking for you earlier.'

'I gather you've had some details about our new CO.' As she spoke Helen sat down in one of the two chairs facing Elliot's desk and, easing off her shoe, began to rub her foot.

'Swollen ankles?' Elliot raised his eyebrows but his tone wasn't unsympathetic.

'No.' Helen shook her head. 'New shoes. I made the mistake of wearing them for the first time when I was in London. I should have known better. I don't think my feet will ever recover.'

'Talking of London,' said Elliot, 'I thought I would arrange a couple of lectures for some time next week so that you can pass on what you learnt while it's still relatively fresh in your mind.'

'Er...I made pretty extensive notes, actually,' said Helen. Briefly she wondered what Elliot would say if he knew that she could hardly remember a single thing she'd heard at any of the lectures.

'Oh, well done.' He began to shuffle some papers on his desk. 'Now, what was the other thing I wanted to tell you?' He looked harassed for a moment.

'The new CO?' she said helpfully.

'Oh, yes.' He looked relieved. 'That was it. My memory just doesn't seem to be what it was. Well, they've appointed someone and for once he's able to start immediately—as soon as Andrew leaves, in fact, which will make life easier for us.'

'Anyone we know?' asked Helen. She was still rubbing her foot, which really did feel quite painful, and she didn't even bother to look up. A new CO on the unit was hardly an earth-shattering event. They came and they went. Some were good and some were not so good.

'Actually,' said Elliot, 'that's the strange part. Yes, as it happens, it is someone we know—or at least someone we've met, even if it was only briefly.'

'Oh, who was that, then?' Helen glanced up.

'You remember at Kate Chapman's wedding—the guy who'd just come back from Timbuctoo or Katmandu or somewhere—Jon Hammond's best man?'

Helen stopped rubbing her foot. 'Yes,' she said. 'What about him?'

'Well, it's him.'

Slowly she slipped her foot back into her shoe. 'What do you mean, it's him?' she said quietly.

'What I say.' Elliot shrugged. 'Apparently, it was mentioned at the wedding that Andrew was leaving and that the CO post would be becoming vacant here. Anyway, I suppose it must have appealed to him because he applied for it. I must admit I was rather surprised. When I spoke to him I got the impression that he was all set to return to wherever it was he'd come from.'

He paused and peered over his glasses. 'I say,' he said, 'are you all right, Helen? You should get that foot seen to if it's giving you that much bother, you know. You look quite pale.'

She wasn't sure how she got out of Elliot's office. All she knew was that the world seemed to have tilted slightly on its axis and that her heart was thumping so hard she was in danger of suffocating.

She stood for a moment outside the office, one hand on the doorframe, as she struggled to regain her equilibrium. There must be some mistake, she told herself at last. Elliot must have been misinformed. There was absolutely no way that Nick Sawyer could be coming here to work.

But could a mistake have been made about something like that? Elliot had had the forms in front of him. Could there be two people by the same name?

Yes, that was it. It had to be that. But two Nick Sawyers who both worked for the VSO and who both had the right qualifications to work in A and E as a CO? That really did seem highly unlikely.

But, if it was him, why hadn't he told her? He must have known all the time they had been together in London. And even if he hadn't known he'd actually got the job, he'd known he'd applied for it.

'Helen! What is it? Whatever's the matter? You look as if you've just seen a ghost.'

She looked up to find Georgina staring at her in obvious concern.

'Oh,' she said faintly, 'oh, it's nothing…'

'It doesn't look like nothing. There's something wrong. I know there is. You haven't been yourself all week, and now…' Georgina trailed off. Glancing at her watch, she said, 'Look, it's time you and I went to lunch. Come on, we'll go to the canteen and you can tell me all about it.'

Somehow Helen didn't have the energy to protest or even to refuse. She felt as if all the stuffing had been knocked out of her, and she allowed Georgina to propel her to a window seat in the canteen where she waited as if in a daze while her friend bought her a packet of salad sandwiches and a carton of fresh orange juice.

'Right,' said Georgina as she sat down opposite Helen and opened her own pack of sandwiches, 'what's this all about?'

'I don't really know where to start,' said Helen faintly, not certain quite how much she wanted Georgina to know.

'Is it Richard?' Georgina leaned forward slightly and looked into her face.

'What?' Helen frowned. Her brain was teeming as she tried to get her chaotic thoughts into some sort of order, but the thought that remained firmly entrenched in the very forefront of her mind was that Nick was coming here. Her one saving grace in the past week had been the fact that she knew she was never going to see him again. Now that had been turned on its head. Not only was she going to see him again, it seemed she was also expected to work with him.

'Richard,' said Georgina again. 'Is this something to do with him?'

'Richard?' repeated Helen blankly. 'Why do you think it's anything to do with him?'

'Well, I just did, that's all,' said Georgina. 'Because lately… Oh, it doesn't matter,' she added hastily as if she'd said more than she'd meant to. 'So it isn't, then? To do with Richard, I mean.'

Helen shook her head. 'No,' she said at last, 'it isn't anything to do with Richard. At least…' She paused.

'Yes?' said Georgina quickly, eagerly almost.

'It isn't anything to do with Richard at the moment…but…but the way things are going…it could well be. Oh, Georgina,' she said suddenly, desperately, 'I don't know what I'm going to do.'

'For goodness' sake, Helen. What is it?' Georgina looked really alarmed now. 'You must tell me.'

'It's…it's about…something that happened in London…'

'I said you've been different since you came back from London,' said Georgina, and there was a touch of satisfaction in her voice as she leaned back in her chair and surveyed Helen thoughtfully.

'And it's about the new CO,' Helen added weakly.

'The new CO?' Georgina's eyes widened slightly with sudden interest. 'It's going be that nice Nick Sawyer. Andrew told me just now…' She paused as she caught sight of Helen's expression. 'Do you have a problem with that, Helen?' she said after a moment. 'I must say we thought he was really nice when we met him at the wedding. And he comes with a first-class reference from Jon Hammond, of course. I think that always helps, don't you, when someone actually knows the person? I gather they were at medical school together then later both worked with the VSO.'

'Yes. And that's where I was given to understand Nick Sawyer was returning after his stint in Norfolk,' said Helen tightly. 'His work with the VSO—in Nepal or wherever it was.'

'I guess he changed his mind,' said Georgina, adding with a frown, 'But I still don't see what the problem is.'

Helen drew a deep breath and made a supreme effort to get herself under control. 'Let's just say it was a shock, that's all, finding out that he was coming here to work.'

'But I don't understand,' Georgina looked bewildered. 'Don't you like him?'

'Let's just say I prefer not to work with him,' said Helen, biting ferociously into her sandwich.

'But you don't know him. How can you possibly know what he's like to work with when you've only met him the once?'

Georgina stared at Helen and when Helen avoided her gaze she set her cup down, her eyes narrowing suspiciously. 'You *have* only met him the once?' she said at last. When Helen didn't reply the truth apparently dawned on Georgina for slowly she said, 'He was in London, wasn't he? At the conference?'

Helen drew a deep breath. 'Yes,' she said at last, 'he was.'

'Did you know he was going to be there?'

'No, of course I didn't,' protested Helen. 'It was a coincidence, that's all.'

'So, what happened?'

Carefully Helen set down the plastic beaker that held her orange juice. 'What do you mean, what happened?'

'Well, something must have happened for you to react

so strongly when you knew he was coming here to work,' said Georgina, staring at her across the table.

'Not necessarily,' said Helen stubbornly. 'You just get to see another side to people on these conferences, that's all. Meeting someone for half an hour at a wedding is one thing—seeing them for a whole week is something else entirely.'

'I take it there were other people at this conference, apart from Nick Sawyer?' Georgina spoke half-jokingly but Helen felt herself stiffen.

'Of course there were,' she said, 'dozens of them.'

'But you saw enough of him to know that you don't like him?'

'I didn't say I didn't like him,' she retorted swiftly. 'I merely said I wouldn't want to work with him, that's all.' She shrugged and when Georgina didn't respond she added, 'There's nothing in that—you know yourself there are those people you could work with and those you couldn't.'

'Don't you think you are being a little unfair to Nick Sawyer?' Georgina's eyes narrowed slightly. 'After all, you haven't as yet even had the pleasure of working with him—maybe he's completely different in the workplace than he appears at a conference.'

'Yes... Maybe...' Helen drained her cup then rose. 'We'd best get back,' she said.

'Are you all right now?' asked Georgina.

Helen nodded. 'Yes,' she said. 'I guess I'm just being silly, that's all.'

'Well, if you do have a problem with the new CO...' Georgina stared up at her and there was still concern in her brown eyes. 'If there *is* a dark side to his nature that only you have caught a glimpse of maybe you'll have to have a word with Elliot.'

'Yes, maybe,' Helen replied quietly.

She didn't know how she was going to get through the rest of that week. She had thought of writing to Nick, begging him not to take up the appointment, but she didn't even have his address so final had been their parting; 'This has to be the end,' she'd told him during that last night together. 'There can be no future for us. This is all we have.' And he'd agreed. At least, he'd appeared to agree.

She had contemplated asking Elliot for his address and risking his curiosity, raiding his briefcase even or going to Jon Hammond and asking him, but she could think of no justifiable reason for any of these moves and in the end she remained silent. Georgina didn't raise the subject again but still seemed concerned about her.

To her dismay, Helen even found herself avoiding Richard, limiting their meetings to nothing more intimate than a lunch and on another occasion an outing with him and his children to the local bowling alley, followed by a visit to McDonald's.

She had steeled herself not to feel any guilt where Richard was concerned over what had happened between herself and Nick, and she had honestly come to believe that she could do it—that the magic of that week could remain simply that for all time, a magical interlude.

But that had been then, when she had thought she would never set eyes on Nick again, before she had known he was coming to the Shalbrooke and into her life once more.

Now it had all changed and she had no idea how she would react when she saw him again, what it would be like to work alongside him day in and day out and what would happen when they met socially, which was inevitable in the small community they lived in. He was a friend of Jon Hammond's, Jon was married to Kate, and Kate was her friend as well as being Richard's partner at the Fleetwood Medical Centre—that their paths would cross at every conceivable opportunity was a foregone conclusion.

And so the week of fear and trepidation lurched on. The only thing that briefly took her mind off what was about to happen was Dot Sharman's visit to her GP.

'So, how did you get on?' she asked Dot the following morning.

'Blood tests, lots of prodding about…' Dot pulled a face '…an urgent referral to the gynae clinic and he's signed me off work until it's all sorted out.'

'And it will be, Dot. Really, it will.' Helen couldn't fail to see the fear in Dot's eyes as she hastened to reassure her.

'I don't like the sound of it,' said Georgina later when she and Helen were rearranging rotas to cover Dot's shift. 'I really don't.'

'Well, at least they are moving fast,' said Helen.

'True,' agreed Georgina. 'Trouble is, we don't know how long Dot kept quiet about it, do we?'

Helen sighed. 'No, I suppose not. Dot's such a private person and she hates any fuss especially if it's directed towards herself.'

'Does she have anyone—at home, I mean?' asked Georgina anxiously. 'I know she's divorced, and that there weren't any children. I knew her as a child but, apart from that, I'm ashamed to say I know very little about Dot's life.'

'She lives alone,' said Helen. 'Her parents are both dead. I think she has a sister who lives in Ryde.'

'So, apart from that, she's alone?'

'Yes. Except for Norman, of course.'

'Norman?' Georgina looked up quickly. 'Oh, you mean our Norman, our porter, Norman Westfield?'

Helen nodded. 'Yes, he adores Dot, you know. I gather she's kept him at arm's length for years. Always said she didn't want to get involved again after her husband left her but, well, maybe now she might realise she needs someone.'

'Everybody needs someone,' said Georgina firmly. 'You made me see that, Helen, when I was being so stubborn over Andrew.' She paused.

Helen, recognising the speculative gleam that came into Georgina's eyes, hastily managed to change the subject. The last thing she wanted was another heart-to-heart with Georgina so soon after the last one. She'd got away with it the last time, but she wasn't sure she could convince her friend a second time that all was well in her world when so clearly it wasn't.

CHAPTER SIX

'Hi!'

It was a single syllable, that was all, and Helen had her back to the person who uttered it, the person who had come quietly into the storeroom where she had been checking supplies and who, even now, was standing behind her.

She didn't have to turn round to see who it was. She knew without looking, would have known Nick's voice anywhere in the world. She knew he had arrived. She had heard Elliot say so and that he was with Susan Joliffe, the other doctor on that particular A and E shift. But she hadn't seen him yet, hadn't come face to face with him or let her eyes meet that look of amusement she'd come to know so well.

Slowly she turned, realising as she did so that not only was her heart thudding uncomfortably but that her mouth had gone dry and the palms of her hands felt quite damp. In her mind she had imagined that he would look different in some way.

But it was the same dark hair, slightly untidy, the classically sculptured features and firm mouth and, yes, there was amusement in those hazel eyes, but there was something else as well—something that seemed to melt her very bones.

She had made up her mind that she would appear slightly cool, even distant at first, then later, when the opportunity arose, she would demand an explanation, while at the same time showing her disapproval over his apparent deceit.

'Helen,' he said softly. His gaze roamed over her, taking in her hair, tied back today and tucked beneath her white cap, her grey eyes, slightly troubled but quite incapable of hiding her feelings, and finally coming to rest on her mouth.

'Nick,' she whispered helplessly. Then her resolve crumbled and she said, 'Why? Oh, why have you come here?'

'Because I had to,' he said quietly, seriously. Lifting his hand, he gently ran the back of his fingers down her cheek. 'Because I couldn't bear to stay away.' The gesture was so tender, so poignant that Helen's breath caught in her throat.

For a long moment they simply stared at each other in a sort of dazed wonder then, at the sound of approaching voices, they were both jolted from their reverie.

'Nick,' she said quietly and urgently, 'I haven't told anyone about…about what happened…'

'I didn't for one moment imagine you would,' he replied, his gaze not leaving hers for a second.

Together they left the storeroom, passing the two nurses whose voices they had heard and who now stared at them in astonishment as, followed by muffled giggles, they made their way to Reception.

Elliot and Georgina were in the nurses' station, and they both looked up as Helen and Nick approached.

'Ah,' said Elliot, 'I see you two have renewed your acquaintance.'

'Yes, we have, thanks,' said Nick easily.

Georgina looked as if she had been about to say something but had thought better of it, but the look she gave

Helen was speculative to say the least. Helen knew there wouldn't be any fooling Georgina, at least not for long.

She was saved for the time being, however, by the growing number of patients in Reception and the need for the morning routine to commence.

Even if she had wished it otherwise, there was no avoiding Nick. He was there beside her throughout the entire morning, his presence evoking all sorts of memories of the brief, ecstatic time they had spent together—his hands as he examined a patient, the way his hair flopped over his forehead when he became engrossed in what he was doing, the way his mouth would twitch slightly when he was about to laugh, and always, always, there was that amusement and humour that lurked in his eyes.

Even when he dragged off his tie and unbuttoned the top buttons of his shirt she found her gaze drawn to the dark tangle of hair just visible beneath, and as more memories were rekindled felt herself shudder with forbidden delight.

By the end of the morning she was almost in despair. This simply couldn't go on. How on earth could she be expected to do her job efficiently under such conditions?

'We need to talk,' she said desperately at last in a fierce whisper as she assisted him in suturing a cut on a young man's hand.

'But of course,' he murmured. 'When do you suggest?'

'The canteen. Lunchtime,' she almost snapped.

'OK,' he replied in a casual way which only served to infuriate her even more. How dare he! How dare he come back here and turn her whole world upside down?

'Why didn't you tell me?' she demanded later over a cup of hot sweet tea which she hoped might be as effective for treating despair as it was reputed to be for the treatment of shock. 'When we were in London, why didn't you say?'

'I didn't know then,' he said helplessly, stirring his tea as if he, too, was conscious of a sudden need to increase his sugar levels.

'What do you mean, you didn't know?' She stared at him, wishing he wasn't so handsome and that his eyes didn't crinkle at the corners the way they did in that maddeningly attractive way. 'You must have known you'd applied for the job.'

'Oh, yes, I knew that, of course I did, but I didn't imagine for one moment that I'd get it so I didn't even bother to mention it.'

'But when did you apply for it, for heaven's sake?' she demanded.

'After the wedding,' he said. 'When it was mentioned that there would be a vacancy here Jon suggested I apply for the job.'

'But why would he do that?' Helen frowned. 'I thought you were all set to go back to Nepal, or wherever it was, for the VSO when your temporary contract finished in Norfolk.'

'Well, yes, that had been the original plan,' he agreed, 'but I happened to mention to Jon that I half envied him the fact that he was settling down and putting down some roots at long last. He told me there was no reason why I shouldn't do the same. So on a wild impulse I applied for Andrew Merrick's job. But, like I say, I didn't think I had a hope in hell of getting it. When I got the letter to say my application had been successful I couldn't believe it.'

'It didn't occur to you to turn it down?' she asked coolly.

He shook his head. 'No,' he said. 'Why should it?'

She stared at him. 'You didn't think it might make life difficult for me?'

'I can't see why it should,' he said calmly. 'After all, you did say you hadn't told anyone about what happened in London, didn't you?'

'I told Georgina that we met in London,' she said slowly. 'That we were at the same conference...'

'But presumably that was all. You didn't tell her anything else?' His eyes widened slowly.

'No,' she said quickly, looking away, suddenly unable to meet his gaze. 'No, of course I didn't.'

'Well, then,' he said quietly, 'I can't see there's any problem.'

She remained very still for a long moment and then, without looking at him, she said, 'There's no way, Nick, that what happened between us can in any way be continued.'

'Well, no. I had already worked that one out,' he said. There was more than a touch of regret in his tone, which Helen did her best to ignore. 'But,' he went on after a moment, 'that doesn't mean we aren't still friends, does it?'

Helen drew in her breath sharply. She wanted to tell him that, no, she couldn't settle for mere friendship between them after what had happened, but something prevented her from doing so. Maybe—and awful as the possibility was, it still had to be considered—it hadn't meant as much to him as it had to her. Maybe it wouldn't in any way be traumatic for him, working alongside her.

'No,' she said at last when it became clear that he was waiting for her answer. 'No, of course it doesn't.'

'Well, that's a relief.' He grinned. 'For one awful moment I thought you were going to say that not only could we no longer be lovers—'

'Nick, shh, please…' She glanced furtively around the canteen but he carried on speaking as if he hadn't heard her.

'But that we couldn't be friends either—and, Helen? I don't think I could bear that.'

'Nick,' she began, but he held up his hand.

'It's OK,' he said with a sigh, 'you don't have to spell it out. I know you have Richard and that your future is all planned out for you, and I promise I won't do anything to mess things up for you but…' He paused and when she looked up—quickly, anxiously—he went on, 'It was good, wasn't it, Helen?'

'What?' She stared at him.

'Between us,' he went on unmercifully. 'It was good. Very, very good.'

She drew another deep breath, 'Yes, Nick,' she agreed at last, 'it was good. But it was in the past. It was a one-off. Probably it should never have happened, but it did. But that's it now. Life has to go on and if we are to work together I don't want there to be any misunderstanding between us.'

'Of course not.' He rose and looked down at her. 'There won't be, Helen, I promise.' He winked at her, then he turned and walked out of the canteen. He had sounded sincere but as Helen watched him go her emotions felt in more of a muddle than ever.

When at last she returned to the unit it was to find Georgina deep in conversation with Elliot. They both looked up as she approached the desk.

'Oh, good,' said Elliot, 'here she is now.'

Immediately Helen stiffened, imagining they had been

talking about her, maybe speculating about her and Nick Sawyer.

'There's an emergency coming in,' said Elliot. 'All hands on deck.'

'Do we know what it is?' asked Helen in relief. She had to stop this, she knew. She was in danger of becoming paranoid, imagining she was the focus of everyone's conversation.

'An accident on a building site somewhere in Cowes,' said Elliot. 'I've already called the duty anaesthetist—he's on his way over. It's Richard Fleetwood, and I've paged the consultant registrar.'

As Helen turned to make her way to the ambulance bay, ready to receive the first casualties, Elliot called her back. 'Oh, there was one other thing, Helen,' he said, 'now that you and Georgina are both here.'

'What's that?' Both Helen and Georgina stopped and looked at him, something in his tone warning them that what he was about to say was serious.

'It's about Dot.' He spoke quietly so that no one else in the vicinity could hear. 'It's just been confirmed,' he went on. 'She has a malignant tumour on one of her ovaries.'

Helen stared at him in dismay. 'Oh, poor Dot,' she said at last. 'Can they operate?'

Elliot nodded. 'Apparently, yes. She's going to Theatre later today for a total hysterectomy.'

'I'll go up and see her after my shift,' said Helen. 'Oh, here we go,' she said as an ambulance suddenly stopped outside with a squeal of brakes. Inside were two very badly injured men from the building site who had fallen to the ground when faulty scaffolding had given way. A third man, who had been underneath the scaffolding at the time of its collapse, had also sustained severe head injuries.

The A and E team swung into action, taking over from the paramedics who had administered first aid and had secured neck braces on the injured men to immobilise them in case of injury to the spine. One of the paramedics was Helen's cousin, Siobhan, but there was barely time for more than a quick greeting as the medical routines were put into operation.

As more and more staff appeared to deal with the emergency Helen found herself working with Susan Joliffe as they assessed the injuries of the first man.

'Looks as if we have a shattered tibia and fibula on his left leg,' said Susan. 'And the talus is so badly splintered that fragments of bone are protruding through the skin on his foot. Make him comfortable please, Sister, then we'll get him to X-Ray.'

While Helen's staff tended to the man she moved across the treatment room to the second patient, who had just been assessed by Nick.

'Both femurs look to be fractured here,' he murmured, glancing up at Helen as she approached. 'And I wouldn't be surprised if his pelvis wasn't as well—but X-rays will confirm. It's all right, old chap,' he said reassuringly, as the man on the bed began to moan with pain. 'We'll give you something for the pain, then we'll see about sorting you out.'

'Sister.' He glanced up at Helen. 'Pethidine, please, for this man.'

Nick waited while Helen drew up the injection, and she was only too aware that he was watching her carefully. Suddenly she had the feeling he was going to say something, possibly something for her ears alone, and she found herself glancing around.

'That paramedic,' he said at last and she relaxed, 'the one with the red hair. Was that Siobhan—the girl you were telling me about?'

'Yes,' she nodded, 'yes, that's Siobhan.'

'She's very attractive,' he observed as he took the syringe from her.

'Yes,' Helen agreed, 'she is.'

'She's also very married.' They both turned and found Georgina behind them.

'So I believe,' said Nick with a smile. 'To another paramedic, I understand?'

'Yes,' Georgina nodded. 'Our Dave Morey—it took red hair and Irish charm to finally tame him.'

'Lucky man.' Nick swiftly administered the injection and handed back the empty syringe to Helen. 'It must run in the family,' he said a moment later.

'What?' Georgina frowned.

'Beauty and charm,' Nick replied, with a smile at Helen.

She felt her cheeks grow warm and, only too aware of Georgina's expression, she moved smartly away to check on the third patient. This was the man who had sustained the head injuries. He was severely concussed and was to be the first of the three to go to Theatre.

'I would say there's a chance he'll have to be airlifted to Southampton to the neurological department,' said Nick. 'I don't think we'll have the facilities here to cope with an injury like that.'

At last the routine assessments were completed, X-rays taken and results discussed with the consultant orthopaedic surgeon, and a general surgeon before all three men prepared for Theatre.

Helen had just returned to the nurses' station, where

Susan Joliffe and Nick were still discussing the X-rays, when Richard arrived.

'Hello, there,' he said when he caught sight of Nick, then, in his usual absent-minded fashion, he said, 'I know your face, but I'm afraid I can't put a name to it.'

'Nick Sawyer.' Nick stepped forward and held out his hand. 'We met at Jon's and Kate's wedding.'

'Of course we did.' Richard shook his hand. 'Helen did tell me you were coming. Andrew's replacement, aren't you?'

Nick nodded. 'Yes, that's right.'

'Permanent, are you?' He spoke conversationally but Helen found herself holding her breath as she waited for Nick's reply. Incredibly, she realised at that moment that was one question she hadn't thought of asking, yet it was a question whose answer could have great significance.

'No, only a temporary contract,' said Nick. 'Three months.'

Three months. Three months was quite a long time. On the other hand, it would soon pass. Then what? He would go. But surely that was what she wanted. Wasn't it? For him to go so that she could get on with the rest of her life?

'Where are you living?' Richard was talking again and suddenly, unreasonably, she wanted to tell him to shut up, go off to Theatre to do what he had come to do and stop interfering.

'I've only just arrived,' said Nick, 'and for the moment I'm with Jon and Kate.'

'That's nice,' said Richard. 'Lovely apartment they have. Wonderful views of the Solent. You a sailing man?' he asked.

'Afraid not,' said Nick.

'Oh, well, never mind.' Richard said it as if he couldn't understand anyone who didn't sail. 'You can still appreciate the views, I dare say.'

'Yes, quite,' said Nick, 'although it's not a situation I can take advantage of.'

Richard had been about to move on but he paused and looked back. 'How do you mean?' he said.

'I shall have to look for somewhere else.'

'Oh, really?' The slightly vague look was back on Richard's face again. 'And why's that?'

'I'm not too good at playing gooseberry.'

'Playing gooseberry? Oh, oh, I see what you mean.' Richard's frown cleared and he gave a guffaw of laughter. 'Newly-weds and all that. So, what will you do?'

'Oh, I shall look round for something—a flat or an apartment.' Nick shrugged. 'I shouldn't imagine it would be too difficult to find something at this time of the year. If not, I can always settle for hospital accommodation.'

Helen, listening to this exchange, anticipated Richard's next remark even before it had left his lips.

'Oh,' he said, 'we can't have that. Helen has a flat, don't you, Helen?' He turned to her, not giving her a chance to answer, and swept on. 'She lets it out. In fact, Jon Hammond stayed there for a while when he first came to the Island, then what's-her-name, the little Irish girl, Siobhan, was there for a while...but that was before she married young Morey. It's empty now, though, isn't it, Helen?' His enthusiasm at having apparently solved someone's dilemma was only too apparent.

'Yes, Richard,' she said trying to stay calm, 'it is empty, but—'

'Perfect solution, then,' said Richard. 'Looks like you've got yourself a new tenant, Helen.'

'Maybe,' said Nick, 'Helen doesn't want another tenant.'

'Oh, but she does,' said Richard. 'You were only saying as much the other day, weren't you, Helen?'

'I—'

'That's settled, then,' said Richard. 'Now, I must get on. Helping others is all very well, but it does hold one up. Oh, one other thing, old man. Bonfire and firework party at my place. Friday night. You're very welcome to come. Helen will give you all the details.' With a nod to them all he strode off to the scrub room.

Helen was so dismayed that she couldn't bring herself even to look at Nick, but as she turned away she inadvertently caught Georgina's eye. Georgina, who had quietly witnessed the entire conversation.

The remainder of the shift was frantic with no further opportunity for discussion between Helen and Nick. As the shift came to an end Helen wasn't sure whether she was grateful or disappointed.

In the end she left Nick in Theatre, where he was assisting the consultant, and fled out of A and E upstairs to the gynae ward. She met Norman Westfield, who was coming out.

'Hello, Sister.' He nodded, but his usual, cheery smile was missing.

'How is she?' Helen glanced anxiously into the ward.

'Frightened,' said Norman bluntly.

'Has she had her pre-med yet?' asked Helen.

'No, they said in about half an hour.'

'Then I'd best get on in there,' said Helen. 'That is, if Sister will let me. Who's on duty?'

'Sister Graham,' Norman replied then as Helen would

have hurried on, he said, 'Please, Sister, try and reassure her, won't you?'

'I'll try, Norman,' said Helen gently.

'She seems to have got it into her head that she isn't going to come round from the anaesthetic,' he said.

'I'll do my best, Norman.'

After a quick word with the ward sister Helen hurried into a ward, bright with the last of the day's sunshine and filled with the colours of autumn.

'Hello, Dot.' She smiled at her friend, concerned to see traces of tears on her cheeks.

'Oh, Helen, it's you.' Bravely Dot attempted a smile. 'I had to send Norman away. He was getting upset and he was making me upset as well.'

'It's only because he cares about you so much,' said Helen, as she pulled up a chair and sat beside the bed.

'I know,' said Dot. She gulped. 'And do you know something else? It's taken this for me to see that. I didn't want to believe it before.'

'Perhaps it was a case of once bitten twice shy?' said Helen.

'After Ken, you mean?' Dot nodded. 'Yes, I suppose you could be right. My marriage was such a disaster and I felt such a failure, as if it was all my fault. I wouldn't let Norman into my life. I was afraid, you see, afraid it would all go wrong again.'

'Norman is very different from Ken, Dot,' said Helen.

'I know.' Dot took a peach-coloured tissue from a box on her locker and blew her nose. 'Ken was a brute, Helen. I have to face that, and I know Norman isn't like that. He is so gentle, he wouldn't hurt a fly, and I know he loves me...but...I've never given him the chance to prove it. Now I may have left it too late...'

'Of course you haven't,' said Helen firmly. 'You'll

get this op out of the way then you'll be as good as new.'

'There'll be treatment.' Dot dabbed her eyes again. 'I'm not sure I can face all that, Helen, the radiotherapy, possibly chemotherapy, losing my hair...'

'You won't be alone, Dot. Norman will be right there beside you, helping you through it all. And the rest of us are all rooting for you.'

'I know... I know...' Dot gave a great shuddering sigh.

'You're going to be just fine,' said Helen. 'I know you are. Besides, it's time we had another wedding,' she added drily. 'It's all of a month since the last.'

'I thought you were going to be next,' said Dot, dropping her soggy tissue into the wastebin and reaching for another.

'Oh, I don't know about that,' said Helen. She spoke lightly, almost flippantly, but was momentarily shocked to discover that when Dot had mentioned the possibility of her own wedding and had, no doubt, been referring to Richard, it had not been Richard's name or image that had come into her mind but Nick Sawyer's.

Firmly she dismissed the image which she knew, if allowed to linger, would grow into a fantasy that would quickly become out of control.

'Hasn't Dr Fleetwood asked you yet?' said Dot curiously, her own troubles apparently forgotten for the moment.

Helen laughed. Somehow it was impossible to take offence at Dot. 'Actually,' she said, 'no, he hasn't—at least, not in so many words.'

'Well, he wants to get a move on—life's too short to mess about.' As she realised what she had said Dot's eyes filled with tears again.

Hastily, to change the subject or maybe because of the nature of the conversation he was on her mind, Helen said, 'Dot, you remember the best man at Kate's wedding?'

Dot sniffed and nodded. 'How could I forget? The Mel Gibson look-alike?'

'Yes, that's him.' Helen smiled. 'Well, he's our new CO.'

'You're joking!' Dot stared at her in amazement.

'No. He's taken Andrew Merrick's place.'

'Well! If that's not an incentive to get out of here, I don't know what is.' Dot paused. 'What's he like—apart from his looks, I mean.

Helen swallowed. 'He's very nice,' she said.

'Well, that's good,' said Dot. 'The trouble with these very good-looking types is that they usually know it.'

'Oh, no,' Helen heard herself say. 'Nick Sawyer isn't a bit like that.'

At that moment a staff nurse appeared, a kidney dish and syringe in one hand. 'Time for your pre-med, Dot,' she said, as she began to draw the curtains around the bed.

'I must go.' Helen stood up. 'I'll be back to see you tomorrow, Dot,' she said.

'Yes. OK.' Dot's smile was still tremulous but at least she had stopped crying.

CHAPTER SEVEN

'It's completely out of the question,' Helen told Nick later on her return to her office to collect her coat, before leaving for home.

'So you don't want another tenant?' He followed her and stood with one hand on the doorframe, watching her as she shut down her computer and locked her desk.

'I didn't say that,' she replied quietly, trying to remain calm. 'As it happens, yes, I was looking for another tenant. The flat has been empty since Siobhan left and it's company for me having someone close by, especially now that my father is no longer there.'

'So it's just this particular tenant you object to, is that it?' The humour was back in his eyes and she quickly looked away, afraid she might give in—that the temptation might prove too great.

'Yes,' she said quietly, 'and you know why.'

'What do we tell Richard?' he asked innocently.

'What do you mean?' She threw him a sharp glance, then took her coat from a hook behind the door.

'Well, he seems to be under the impression it's all settled.' Nick moved into the room as he spoke and took her coat to help her into it, accidentally—or possibly deliberately—allowing his fingers to brush her nape.

She stiffened at his touch, something she'd yearned for ever since their parting. 'Leave Richard to me,' she murmured.

'What will you say?' he said softly, his mouth very close to her ear.

'I don't know.' There was a note of desperation in her voice now. 'Something, anything. I'll say the flat was too small...yes, that's it. It was too small.'

'In that case, don't you think I should at least see this flat if I am to form an opinion like that?'

'I don't see that it's necessary.'

'Well, I do,' he replied calmly. 'What will I say to Kate and to Jon when they ask, as no doubt they will after they've spoken to Richard? How can I tell them that the flat was unsuitable, too small, when I haven't even seen it?'

'You could pretend you've seen it,' she said desperately.

'Oh, I don't think so,' he replied. 'They might ask me something about it. I don't think I could carry it off if I hadn't actually seen it.'

'Oh, very well,' she said at last in exasperation. 'You'd better come and see it, I suppose, but on the strict understanding that when you do so you reach the conclusion that it's completely unsuitable for your requirements.'

'Of course.'

'You'd better follow me,' she said. 'I don't suppose you know where Gatcombe is?'

'No,' he replied innocently, 'I don't. There is, however, one small problem.'

'Oh?' By this time she was following him from the office and as she turned to shut the door he stopped and waited for her.

'I'm afraid I don't have any transport.'

'Well, that's another reason why you couldn't live at the flat,' said Helen briskly as they walked down the corridor into Reception. 'Gatcombe is in the heart of the country so you would need your own transport—you couldn't rely on public transport to get you to work, not with the shifts we do.'

'But I would have you,' he said softly. 'We more or less work the same hours so surely it would make sense to travel together.'

She opened her mouth to protest. This whole thing seemed to be spinning totally out of control. She closed it again as Elliot came out of his office and peered at the two of them over his glasses.

'Survived your first day, then, Nick?' he said.

'Yes, I think so,' Nick replied with a laugh. 'One A and E department is very much like another in my experience.'

'You're right.' Elliot nodded. 'Can I give you lift? I'm going through Cowes.'

'Thanks all the same,' Nick replied, 'but I'm going to have a look at Helen's flat.'

'Oh, yes,' said Elliot. 'Richard said something about that. I think it would be ideal for you. And you and Helen would be able to travel together as well—a good arrangement all round, I would say.'

'I wish,' said Helen tightly as she and Nick headed for the car park, 'that everyone would stop trying to run my life for me. I'm getting just a bit tired of people sorting things out and jumping to conclusions.'

'I guess folks are only trying to be helpful,' said Nick as they reached her car. He waited as she unlocked the doors then slid into the passenger seat beside her.

As she put her key into the ignition, after fastening her seat belt, Helen found that her hands were shaking, and as she drew out of the car park the incongruity of the situation finally hit her.

She had fought her feelings for Nick ever since that unbelievable week they had spent together and had tried to make it all go away, to pretend almost that it had never happened. Only now she found herself with him, here beside her in her car—having spent the day working alongside him—travelling to her home to look at her flat with a view to him becoming her new tenant. And this at the instigation of the man she believed that one day she would marry and with whom she'd spend the rest of her life.

She had to wait to give way to another car, only to find that it was driven by Georgina who paused when she saw the pair of them together, raised her eyebrows, smiled and waved.

'Damn,' muttered Helen under her breath.

'What's up?' asked Nick as he waved back to Georgina.

'That was the last thing I needed,' said Helen tightly.

'What do you mean?'

'For Georgina to see us, driving away together,' she replied. 'She's been giving me funny looks all day.'

'Do you think she suspects anything?' asked Nick, as they drove out of the hospital grounds and joined the main road.

'There's nothing to suspect,' said Helen, and because she was feeling a little fraught it came out more sharply than she had intended.

'Sorry,' said Nick. After a moment he added, 'I just thought that because you said you'd told her that we'd met each other in London, and that she'd been giving you funny looks all day, she might read something into the fact that we are driving off together, that's all.'

Helen didn't answer, concentrating instead on her driving as she drove away from Shalbrooke and approached the Newport road.

'Lovely countryside,' he said after a while as they

bypassed Newport and travelled through a network of country lanes. It was almost dusk, the autumn colours muted now, but high on its hill the stark battlements of Carisbrooke Castle were sharply etched against a turquoise sky.

'Yes,' said Helen. 'I never tire of that scene.'

'The Island is bigger than I imagined,' said Nick a little later as they approached Gatcombe.

'Most visitors say that when they see it for the first time,' said Helen as she turned the car off the road and into a narrow lane. 'People think they can walk round the entire perimeter in a day and are amazed when they find they can't.'

'The "Coach House",' Nick read as they passed the white, painted sign. 'So this is home.'

'Yes,' Helen nodded, 'this is home.' She brought the car to a halt in front of the large stone house with its ivy-covered walls beneath a slate roof and to one side the dark mass of the stables and coach-house buildings.

While Helen unlocked the front door Nick stood and looked around, drawing in great lungfuls of the evening countryside air. As the door swung open Chester rushed out to greet them, his tail wagging ecstatically.

'Hello, old boy.' Nick bent down to pat the dog as he rushed from one to the other like some demented creature. 'What a welcome!' He laughed. 'Do you get this every evening?'

'Yes,' Helen smiled. 'More so since Dad died.'

'Does he have to stay on his own all day?' asked Nick as Chester rushed by them into the house then charged out again.

'No.' Helen shook her head. 'My neighbour down at the farm, the one who looked after him while I was in London, comes up and takes him for a run around lunchtime. The rest of the time I think he sleeps—he's getting very old now, believe it or not, even though he still insists on behaving like a puppy.'

She led the way into the house as she was speaking and Nick followed her through the hall, down a passage and into the kitchen, where she switched on the light and unlocked and opened the back door. Immediately Chester rushed out into the garden. They stood for a moment and watched him as he ran around the small courtyard then further out into the garden where he disappeared into a dark line of trees and bushes.

Nick, standing behind her, was so close he was almost touching her, and once again Helen felt something close to despair. It would be so easy to unbend, to turn and slip into his arms, but she knew if she did so she would be lost. It would be best to just get on with what he had come for, then he could go, leaving her alone, and the danger would be past.

'Perhaps,' she said, turning slightly, 'you'd like to see the flat now—'

'Why did you go, Helen?' he said, and his voice was low and intense.

She felt herself stiffen again involuntarily, like an animal that scented danger, her body so tense it seemed her bones might snap under the pressure.

'What do you mean?' Her voice came out hoarse, barely more than a whisper.

'In London,' he said. 'That morning. When I woke up you'd gone. I can't describe what I felt at that moment. After the night we'd just spent—I simply couldn't believe it. It was as if you'd died.'

'I thought it for the best,' she said. 'I couldn't bear to say goodbye. At the time I thought it was to be for ever. I don't know how I got home. I kept seeing people I thought were you...and the pain when I discovered they weren't was indescribable. I'm sorry, Nick. I thought...I thought... Oh, I don't know what I thought.'

'I was afraid it hadn't meant as much to you as it had to me.'

'Oh, Nick, if only you knew.' Suddenly she felt his hands on her shoulders and from somewhere she summoned the power to resist him. 'No,' she said firmly. 'I didn't let you come here for this.'

Drawing swiftly away from him but only too aware of his sigh, she led the way out of the back door and into the courtyard where she hardly even waited to make sure that he'd followed before she hurried across to the dark shape of the stable block and switched on the outside light.

Immediately the whole area was suffused with light and she led the way up an iron staircase that ran up the side of the stable block to a small landing where she unlocked the main door to the flat.

'Well, it is small,' he said, as he looked around the living room and kitchen then prowled through the two bedrooms and bathroom and back to join Helen where she waited in the living room, 'but, I have to say, it would be more than adequate for my needs.'

Helen chose to ignore his remarks and, after locking the flat again, they made their way back to the house. She still wanted him to go because she couldn't trust herself if they were alone together for too long, while at the same time, perversely, she longed for him to stay, take her in his arms again and make love to her just as he had before.

'Would you like a drink?' she asked, remembering her manners as they reached the kitchen door. She hoped he would refuse, yet also dreaded that he might.

'Thank you, that would be nice.' He followed her into the kitchen once more and sat down at the pine table.

'What would you like? Tea? Coffee?'

'I don't suppose you have a beer?' He glanced hopefully towards the fridge.

'I have some lager, as it happens.' She didn't mention she kept if for when Richard visited.

'That would be great.' He leaned back in his chair, linked his hands behind his head and gazed around. 'This is a fantastic place,' he said. Have you always lived here?'

'Most of my life, yes,' she replied, as she took a can of lager from the fridge, together with a bottle of wine that she'd opened the night before. 'I was brought up here. I went away to do my training but I came back here afterwards and kept house for my father.'

'You quite obviously love it here,' he said, as she poured his lager into a glass and handed it to him.

'Yes, I do.' She nodded. 'I don't see how anyone could not like it, really.'

'Will you stay here...now?' He watched her carefully as she poured her wine and sat down opposite him at the table.

'Now that my father's gone, you mean?' When he nodded she said, 'I don't know, probably not.'

'You have a sister—is the property half hers?'

She shook her head. 'No, my father left the house to me. He left my sister his portfolio of stocks and shares.'

'So you could stay here?'

'Oh, yes, I could stay here,' she agreed, then she hesitated.

'But Richard wouldn't want to live here—is that what you're saying?'

She shrugged. 'Something like that, yes. He has a

house already, you see, Fleetwood House at Newtown—
that's his family home.'

'Presumably where he lived with his late wife?'

'Yes.' Helen nodded but added hastily, 'Although that
isn't the reason. It's his children. The house is
ideal...but you'll see it for yourself when you come to
the bonfire party. That is, if you intend coming?'

'Of course,' he said softly. 'I wouldn't miss it for the
world.'

She swallowed. 'We shall have to be very careful,
Nick,' she said.

'In what way?' He raised his eyebrows as he took a
sip of his drink but, to Helen's discomfort, the amusement was back in his eyes.

'Well, in that we don't let anything slip...for example,
like how well we know each other.'

'Oh, I thought you meant about not letting anyone
know we were having an affair,' he said.

'But we aren't.' She stared at him in sudden consternation.

'Aren't we?' That expression was back in his eyes
again, the one guaranteed to melt her bones.

'No, Nick,' she said firmly. 'We aren't.'

At that moment the phone rang and in exasperation
she lifted the receiver. 'Hello?' she said. 'Oh, Kate, it's
you,' she added, as she heard her friend's voice at the
other end of the line.

'Hello, Helen,' said Kate. 'Is Nick Sawyer with you?'

'Yes.' Helen paused and stared at Nick across the table as questioningly he raised his glass. 'Yes, he is, actually.'

'Oh, good. He's seen the flat, then. Richard told us
this afternoon that he's going to take it. That's marvel-

lous, isn't it? It's worked out so well now that Siobhan has moved into Dave's flat.'

'Actually, Kate,' said Helen, trying to remain calm, 'Nick hasn't decided about the flat yet.'

'Oh?' She could hear the surprise in her friend's voice. 'Why's that?'

'Well, he wondered if it was a bit small—'

'Small?' Kate interrupted. 'How much space does he need, for heaven's sake? It was perfectly adequate for Jon. He was more than comfortable there.'

'Well, yes, but, well, there's also the question of transport—'

'Transport? Well, presumably he'll get his own car,' said Kate in her usual down-to-earth manner, 'and, let's face it, Helen, in the meantime he can always travel to and fro with you, can't he?'

'I suppose so…'

'You were looking for another tenant, weren't you?'

'Yes.'

'I thought you were. Well, you couldn't do better than Nick, Helen. Really, you couldn't. He's a smashing chap, he really is. Jon's known him for years so you need have no worries there.'

'Oh, yes, I know all that,' said Helen weakly.

'So it's settled, then?'

'Well, I guess it's up to Nick really,' she heard herself say.

'Let me speak to him,' said Kate.

Helplessly Helen passed the phone to Nick. 'Kate wants to speak to you,' she said.

'Hello, Kate?' he said.

Helen watched as he listened to what was quite obviously a tirade from Kate, then at last he said, 'Well, that's that, then. How can I argue with that?'

Frantically she tried to catch his eye, gesticulating that he should refuse, should stand firm, but before she knew what was happening he'd said goodbye to Kate and had hung up.

He turned to her and gave an apologetic shrug. 'Sorry about that,' he said.

'What?' She was aware that a shrill note had crept into her voice.

'Well, there wasn't much I could do, really.'

'What do you mean?' She stared at him.

'It seems Kate and Jon have it all sewn up, and Richard as well, really. I tried to argue, but when Kate turned round and said they all felt it was for the best for you to have someone on the premises how could I argue?'

'I don't understand. Why should Kate say that?' demanded Helen in bewilderment.

'Apparently, they've been concerned about you since you've been on your own. They all seem to think it's too isolated out here for you. So it seems, Helen, my love, I've been assigned to protect you from any evil that might befall you.' Once more he raised his glass while Helen stared at him in dismay.

In the end it seemed the decision had been taken right out of her hands, with everyone else reaching the conclusion as to what was best for her. Helen knew that had she really objected to having Nick Sawyer as a tenant she could have put her foot down, even explaining her reasons to Kate and the others. But there was still a part of her, no matter how much she strove to hide it, that could think of nothing better than having him living in such close proximity.

Even the thought of it carried a thrill of excitement,

an edge of danger that she'd never before experienced. That it would cause all kinds of complications and problems she had little doubt, but because it had not been of her doing she found herself almost washing her hands of the whole affair, inclined to think she could blame her friends if things went wrong—as they undoubtedly would.

'All right if I move my gear in tonight?' asked Nick the following morning as they both stood outside A and E, awaiting the arrival of an ambulance carrying a patient who had suffered a heart attack.

'Why not?' said Helen flippantly. 'Make yourself at home—and anyone else you can think of. The more the merrier!'

'Helen.' The humour disappeared momentarily from his eyes. 'Are you really upset about this?'

'Upset? No. Why should I be? I'm used to other people deciding what is or isn't best for me.' She shrugged, her attitude still frivolous. Catching sight of his expression, she said, 'Well, what do you think, Nick?'

When he looked just a little shamefaced and failed to reply she carried on, but this time without the sharp edge to her voice, 'I just don't think it's wise, that's all. Not after what happened. We're just asking for trouble.'

'I won't take advantage of the situation,' he said quietly, as the awaited ambulance swung into the hospital grounds, its blue light flashing. 'I promise I'll behave.'

'You'll have to, Nick,' she said, and there was a touch of desperation in her voice. 'There will be house rules and you'll simply have to abide by them.'

'What sort of house rules?' He looked faintly startled as the ambulance screeched to a halt and Dave Morey leapt from the driver's seat.

'You stick to your house and I'll stick to mine,' she muttered out of the side of her mouth.

'Oh, I see...' He gave a chuckle, then turned his attention to the situation in hand. He said to Dave, 'Hello, there, what have you got for us?'

'Hi, Doc, Helen,' said Dave, as he opened the rear doors of the ambulance, revealing a second paramedic and a man lying on the stretcher bed. 'Patient suffered an MI at home, then he arrested. His GP defibbed him. How is he now, Greg?'

'Stable,' replied the second paramedic. 'Blood pressure is low but his breathing is easier.'

'Right,' said Helen, 'let's get him inside, shall we, lads?'

Swiftly they wheeled the patient into Reception and through into the first of the unit's two treatment rooms, where they were met by Georgina and Denise. Between them they transferred the patient from the stretcher trolley to the bed, and the nursing team carried out their observations, checking blood pressure and pulse rate, while the two paramedics folded their blankets and packed up the stretcher.

'Thanks, Dave,' said Helen. 'And you, Greg. Well done.'

'Our pleasure.' Dave grinned.

'Siobhan all right?' asked Helen as a matter of course. She expected Dave to say that, yes, his wife was fine, and to move on to return to his ambulance. Instead, he paused and hesitated, before answering.

'She is all right, isn't she?' asked Helen anxiously.

'Er...yes, yes, she's OK...um, perhaps you could give her a ring later, Helen.'

She stared at Dave and noticed to her amazement, that he was blushing. It was such an unusual occurrence to see Dave Morey blush that even Georgina noticed. Dave mumbled something incoherent then, with his head down, he strode from the treatment room.

Greg, Dave's fellow paramedic, gave a helpless shrug. 'He's been like that all day,' he said with a grin. 'Can't get any sense out of him.'

'Do you think it could be what I think it might?' asked Georgina, while even Nick looked up from examining the patient.

'Well, I suppose it could be,' said Helen slowly. 'They've been married all of two months.'

'Good for them,' said Nick. 'There's nothing like a baby for putting the final seal on a marriage.' As he said it his eyes met Helen's, forcing her to look away. 'Don't you agree, Sister Turner?' he added.

'Yes, Dr Sawyer. Absolutely,' Helen replied crisply, aware of Georgina's interested look. 'I certainly hope that's all it is. We have enough to worry about with Dot at the moment, without anyone else giving cause for concern.'

'Talking of Dot,' said Georgina. 'Has anyone heard how she is this morning?'

Helen nodded. 'Yes, Elliot rang the ward. The op was a success, apparently, and the surgeon is pretty certain they've removed all the tumour. I shall be going up to see her at the end of the shift.'

'I'll wait, then, if that's all right with you,' said Nick. 'That is, if you don't mind giving me a lift home.'

'What about your belongings?' she asked sharply.

'Oh, I've got them with me,' he replied. 'Jon gave me a lift this morning. It made sense somehow, seeing we had agreed I could move in.'

Suddenly it became impossible even to look at Georgina, fearing that she simply wouldn't be able to cope with what she saw in her friend's eyes. So Helen fled—out of the treatment room and into the comparative sanctuary of her office where, with her eyes closed, for a long moment she leaned against the door.

CHAPTER EIGHT

HELEN found Dot still very drowsy from the anaesthetic but—in spite of an intravenous drip, a catheter and a drain from the wound site—in remarkably good spirits.

'Mr McGee was very pleased with how the op went,' she murmured as Helen leaned over the bed to hear what she was saying. 'He says he's pretty sure he's got it all.'

'Why do you think we're celebrating downstairs?' said Helen with a smile.

'Are you?' Dot's eyelids began to close again. 'What, everyone?'

'Yes, everyone,' said Helen.

'Even Mel Gibson?'

'Even Mel Gibson.'

'Wow!' mumbled Dot, as she gave up the battle and her eyes finally closed. 'Fancy that.'

'I wonder what you'll say when you know where he's living?' murmured Helen, picking up her friend's hand where it lay on the bedspread and giving it a squeeze.

As she left the gynae ward she met Norman Westfield on his way in, and after one look at his anxious expression she hastened to reassure him. 'She's fine, Norman,' she said. 'Really, she is.'

'Will she have to have more treatment?' he asked doubtfully.

'Probably,' said Helen, 'but that's all to the good, you know.'

'Even if she loses her hair?'

'Don't you think that's a small price to pay for peace of mind?' said Helen gently.

'Yes, I suppose so.' Norman ran his hand ruefully over his own thinning hair. 'Yes, of course, it is. When she comes out,' he went on hesitantly, 'she's going to need some convalescence, isn't she?'

'For a time, yes, she will,' agreed Helen.

'She doesn't really have anyone, you know,' said Norman, 'except for her sister, and she's got three kids to look after. She won't come and stay with me, I know she won't. Besides, I'm at work all day but, well, my sister over at Yarmouth has offered to have her—just for a couple of weeks. Do you think she'd go?' he asked anxiously, his forehead puckered into a deep frown.

'I think you should certainly ask her,' said Helen. 'But if I were you I would leave it a day or so, Norman—she's very tired at the moment.' She watched him as he made his way into the ward, then with a little sigh made her own way down the corridor to the stairs.

Nick was waiting for her in Reception. By his side was a large leather suitcase and two bulky canvas hold-alls.

'I see you're ready,' she said. 'Is that it?' She nodded at the pile of luggage.

'Yep.' He grinned. 'With all my worldly goods I thee endow.'

She glanced around. 'You'll have people getting the wrong impression,' she said.

'Oh, I don't know...' He laughed, and when Helen threw him a sharp glance he held up his hands as if to fend her off. 'Sorry...on second thoughts perhaps I'd better rephrase that.'

Shaking her head, she led the way out of the building to her car where she opened the boot to allow him to stow his luggage inside. Moments later they were in the car and heading for Gatcombe.

'This has all happened so suddenly,' said Helen, 'that I haven't really had time to get the flat ready.'

'It looked all right to me,' said Nick.

'I usually like to make up the bed, that sort of thing…' She trailed off abruptly, knowing as soon as the words left her lips that she'd said the wrong thing.

'Well, that's no problem. I can do that or, if you insist, maybe you could help.' He was laughing now and Helen bit her lip. She had suspected from the start that it was a dreadful mistake to let Nick live in the stable flat, and each passing moment only seemed to reinforce that suspicion.

When they arrived at the Coach House she gave Nick the keys to the flat, and while she fed Chester, before letting him out to run in the garden, Nick took himself off to unpack his belongings and get himself settled in. When she could find no further justifiable excuse for putting it off any longer Helen made her way across the courtyard and climbed the wrought-iron staircase to the flat above.

She tapped on the door and pushed it open. She could hear Nick moving around in the bedroom. For a long moment she hesitated in the kitchen, reluctant to call out, knowing that if she did so he would call her through into the room where he was to sleep. In the end she was saved from making a decision when Nick suddenly appeared in the doorway.

'Oh,' he said, 'sorry. I didn't know you were there.'

'It's OK,' said Helen, wishing he didn't look quite so handsome. He'd taken off his jacket, discarded his tie and rolled up the sleeves of his shirt. His hair was slightly dishevelled and this, together with the dark

shadow on his jaw, gave him an earthy, sexy look that
evoked memories in Helen's mind, memories that were
best left alone, undisturbed, where they could do no further harm.

She swallowed. 'I was just wondering,' she said avert-
ing her gaze from his, 'whether you'd found the sheets
and towels and things.'

'Not yet,' he replied. 'Maybe you'd better stay and
show me where they are.'

'They're through here.' She brushed past him, her
shoulder touching his chest as he made no attempt to
move. 'In the airing cupboard in the bathroom.'

He followed her and simply watched as she opened
the door, stretching up to the top shelf to reach the neatly
folded piles of sheets, duvet covers and towels. As she
lifted them down suddenly he was right there behind her.

'Here,' he said, 'let me take those.' He relieved her
of the pile of bedding and then—even afterwards she
wasn't quite certain how it had happened—the sheets fell
in a heap on the bathroom floor, she ended up in Nick's
arms and before she even had the chance to protest his
mouth had come down on hers.

She tried to struggle and push him away, every in-
stinct warning her that this was sheer madness, but as
desire flared deep inside her and her body responded to
the familiarity of his touch she stopped her resistance.
As the fight went out of her she gave herself up to the
pure pleasure of being in his arms once again.

It felt so right, yet at the same time it was wrong—
she knew that. It shouldn't be happening, it was just
what she had feared would happen, but somehow she
seemed totally powerless to stop either Nick or herself.
And he certainly had no such inclinations as his hands
roamed over her body—moulding her hips, spanning her

waist, caressing her buttocks—drawing her closer and closer.

'Helen,' he groaned against her hair. 'Oh, God, how I've longed for this… The last two days have been sheer hell, being close to you and not being able to touch you.'

'But we mustn't, Nick. This is why it's so wrong for you to be here. I knew this would happen—' She gasped, silenced as he caught her face between his hands and kissed her again, his kiss forceful and demanding as he parted her lips, probing as if he couldn't get enough of her.

'Why can't we?' he demanded, as she began to struggle to try to push him away. 'You want to as much as I do. I know you do.'

'Maybe I do.' Shakily Helen pushed back her hair.

'Then why not? It was good before, wasn't it? You said it was good.'

'Yes,' she whispered. 'Oh, yes, it was good all right.'

'Then why…?'

'Oh, Nick,' she sighed. 'You know why. I told you why. I told you at the time that it was the beginning and the end.'

'I'm still not sure I understand why,' he muttered stubbornly.

'Because of Richard,' she protested.

'Ah, yes, Richard. How could I forget?' He ran a hand through his hair in a hopeless sort of gesture and turned away from her.

'Please try and understand, Nick,' she said desperately. She was finding this difficult enough as it was without his derision. In fact, it was as much as she could do not to give in and let him take her into the bedroom and make love to her just as he had before.

'You say you love Richard?' he demanded at last.

'Of course…' She nodded.

'That you intend marrying him?'

'Yes…'

'So why do I find it so difficult to believe?'

'I don't know. Why do you?' Putting one hand over her mouth, Helen watched him warily.

He gestured helplessly. 'I just do. If I really believed it I guess I might give in gracefully. Heaven knows, I've never been into destroying relationships…but I can't believe it, Helen. I really can't.'

'Don't you think that could be just because you don't want to believe it?' she said.

He shrugged. 'Maybe. I don't know. I just don't find it plausible. Any of it.'

'Richard and I have known each other for a very long time—' Helen began.

'I know. I know all that,' he interrupted. 'I'm sorry, Helen, but there's just something that doesn't seem quite right.'

'I can't betray him,' she said. 'It would be wrong.'

'You aren't married, for heaven's sake,' he replied angrily.

'No, but—'

'So, are you even engaged? Officially, I mean,' he demanded, when she remained silent. 'Do you wear a ring?'

She shook her head. 'No,' she said, then added quickly, 'But that doesn't mean a thing. Not these days.'

'That may be so,' he said quickly, 'but what I'm saying is how sure can you be of any commitment on his part?'

'I just am, that's all. I know him, Nick…' she said helplessly. 'You don't understand.'

He was silent for a long moment, as if wrestling with

some inner conflict, then he gave a deep sigh. 'OK,' he said at last. 'I guess I'm making this very difficult for you. I'm sorry, Helen, truly I am. I just thought that what we had, what we shared, was very special.'

'It was,' she said quickly. 'I'm not denying that.'

'So, what are you saying? That you wish it hadn't happened?'

'No.' She allowed her gaze to meet his again. 'No, Nick, I'm not saying that at all. I'm glad it happened. It probably shouldn't have happened but it did, and because it was so good because it can't be continued it makes it all the harder to bear. And now, with you here…' She shrugged helplessly.

'I shouldn't have come, should I?' he said softly, taking a strand of her hair and winding it around his finger.

'No, Nick,' she said, 'you shouldn't.'

'Do you want me to go? To find somewhere else to live? To give up the job even—to leave the Island?'

'The sensible answer to all of those questions would be yes.' Briefly, helplessly, she rested her head against his chest.

'So…?' he murmured softly against her hair.

'No,' she whispered. 'I don't want you to go.'

'Ah,' he breathed softly.

'On the other hand,' she said quickly, 'I don't want there to be any misunderstanding between us.'

'Oh, of course not,' he said, shocked.

'You will sleep here, Nick, in the flat.'

'But of course.'

'And I will be in the house.'

'That is how I had imagined it would be,' he said solemnly.

She frowned, afraid for a brief moment that she might have misread his intentions and given out the wrong signals. 'We will appear on purely friendly terms at work,' she said, 'and on social occasions…well, I suppose we will just have to see how things go. But I warn you, Nick, if there is any gossip or speculation I will have to ask you to make other arrangements.'

'Absolutely.' He spoke seriously but Helen could sense the suppressed merriment beneath the surface. 'What about meals?' he said a moment later.

'Meals? What about them?' she replied sharply. 'Surely you're not expecting me to cook your meals as well?'

'Of course not. I was simply wondering if we could eat together sometimes, that's all. As it happens, I'm a very good cook so maybe I could cook the odd meal for you.'

'Oh,' she said, slightly taken aback by this unexpected offer. 'Oh, I see. Well, let's just play things by ear for a while, shall we?'

'Why not?' He grinned. 'Now, I really must get my bed made up. Are you going to help me with that?'

'No, Nick,' she replied firmly. 'I really think that is one activity I might live to regret.'

With his laughter still ringing in her ears, she fled out of the flat, down the iron staircase—almost tripping over Chester, who was waiting patiently at the bottom with his nose resting on his paws—and crossed the courtyard to her own home.

She found it difficult to concentrate on very much for the rest of the evening and was just thinking that she might as well give up, have a bath and go to bed when the phone suddenly rang.

'Helen? It's Siobhan.'

She felt a sudden stab of guilt. She should have rung

Siobhan as soon as she'd got home. She had meant to but somehow she had become so caught up in everything that she had quite forgotten. 'How are you, Siobhan?' she asked.

'I'm fine, Helen. I keep being sick, I'm very tired and I seem to spend the best part of each day in the loo but, apart from all that, I'm on top of the world!'

'Oh, Siobhan.' Helen sank down onto one of the kitchen chairs. 'I'm so happy for you. Really, I am.'

'Thanks, Helen. I still can't quite believe it yet—and Dave, well, he's over the moon!'

'Have you told your mum yet?'

'Yes, I phoned her last night. There'll be a big celebration in County Cork tonight.'

'That's wonderful, Siobhan.' A sudden feeling washed over Helen, one she was at a loss to identify—a curious mixture of happiness and envy.

'We hadn't really planned to start a family quite so soon,' Siobhan went on, 'but, well, somehow it just happened, you know how it is...'

'I can imagine,' said Helen with a wry smile. Growing serious again she said, 'You are happy, aren't you, Siobhan?'

'Yes, Helen, truly I am. I've never been more happy in my life.'

'I'm so pleased.'

She was about to ring off when Siobhan suddenly said, 'I understand you've found a replacement for me, Helen.'

'A replacement? Oh, in the flat, you mean?' She swallowed. 'Yes, as it happens, I have.'

'I heard Georgina Merrick talking to one of the other nurses and they said he was drop-dead gorgeous.'

'Well, I don't know about that.' Helen managed a

forced laugh. 'As far as I'm concerned, he's just a tenant.'

'So, who is he exactly?'

'He's a friend of Jon Hammond's—in fact, he was Jon's best man at their wedding.'

'Oh, that's good,' said Siobhan.

'What do you mean?' asked Helen curiously.

'Well, at least you know something about him. You can't be too careful these days who you take into your home.'

'No,' said Helen. 'I suppose not.'

'What's he like, then? Is he as gorgeous as the girls made out?'

'That depends,' said Helen with a laugh, 'on what you call gorgeous. Dot Sharman—you know Dot on A and E?—well, she calls him a Mel Gibson look-alike.'

'Well, now. I must take a look at this new lodger of yours—not that I'm interested, of course,' Siobhan added hastily. 'And I'm sure you aren't either, Helen, because you have Richard.'

'Yes, Siobhan, I have Richard,' she replied.

After she'd replaced the receiver she sat for a long time at the table. She was pleased about the baby, she really was, but the intensity of feeling that had swept over her had startled her. She would have liked children herself, she had always admitted that, but as the likelihood had decreased with each passing year she had gradually come to terms with the fact that motherhood was not to be for her. She knew Richard didn't want any more children and she'd accepted that fact—until now. So what had changed—what had happened to fill her with envy at Siobhan's news and this sudden longing to hold a child of her own?

She knew the answer, without even having to think about it. Nick Sawyer was what had happened.

He had appeared in her life one autumn afternoon and turned her entire world upside down, leaving her in no doubt that things would never be the same again.

Many times during the following week Helen wondered whether she had made the right decision in allowing Nick to stay, whether it wouldn't have been far simpler to tell him that, yes, he should have gone, if not back to the mainland then at least to other accommodation that was well away from her.

It wasn't that he was any trouble, far from it. In fact, he was almost the perfect tenant, quiet, clean and unobtrusive. No, it was quite simply his presence that caused the problem—his close proximity, the forbidden fruit whose very existence became like some exquisite form of torture.

To work alongside him all day was bad enough—hearing his voice, his laughter, watching how others responded to the warmth of his personality, dealing with the occasional accidental touching of hands as they worked, sitting together in the canteen over lunch or beside each other in her car as they travelled to and from the Shalbrooke.

But it was the nights which were the worst—infinitely so—as she lay in her bed, knowing that he was little more than a stone's throw away and that he, too, was in bed.

On more than one occasion she found herself climbing out of bed, drawing back her curtains and gazing across to the dark outline of the stable block. Sometimes the flat was in darkness, at other times his light would be burning. It was then that it was as much as she could do to stop herself from going to him, from simply giving in and begging him to give her the love she so craved.

The only thing that stopped her was Richard—the unspoken understanding that had grown between them, the fact that she had always loved him and that the last thing she wanted to do was to hurt him.

Nick had suggested there was something wrong in her relationship with Richard, but, then, she reasoned, he would say that if what he wanted was to continue what they had started in London. But the idea of a flaw bothered her to such an extent that it began to play on her mind, and she even found herself dreading the thought of the forthcoming bonfire party at Richard's home at Newtown Creek.

'I hate Guy Fawkes celebrations,' said Elliot. 'It was bad enough when it all used to happen on the night of the fifth, but these days they seem to extend it for a week either side.'

'A bit like Christmas, really,' said Georgina.

'You're right.' Elliot looked even more gloomy as he contemplated the next lot of celebrations on the calendar.

'At least the firework activities being staggered has benefits,' said Helen, as she called the next patient from Reception and directed her to a cubicle. 'I can remember A and E being packed out on the fifth of November. Today is the sixth. Last night was quiet, I understand. Are you going to Newtown tonight, Georgina?'

Georgina nodded. 'Yes, Richard has very kindly asked Andrew and me and the children to go.'

'Well, I hope he takes suitable precautions with the fireworks,' said Elliot with a sniff.

'Oh, he does,' said Helen quickly. 'He did this party

last year and the year before that. He has a member of the local fire brigade over to set off the fireworks.'

'I think that is so much more sensible than inexperienced folk letting fireworks off all over the place,' said Georgina, as she and Helen made their way to the cubicle.

The patient requiring treatment was a woman who had apparently had a fall.

'It's Eileen, isn't it?' asked Helen as she closed the curtains behind Georgina and herself.

The woman, who looked very pale, was smartly dressed in a camel coat with a silk scarf at her throat. 'Yes.' She nodded, then bit her lip as if to suppress sudden pain. 'Eileen Clayton.'

'We need to take a few details, Eileen,' said Georgina, opening the file she carried and taking the top off her pen. 'First of all your date of birth and your address, please.'

Eileen Clayton's date of birth showed her to be in her early forties and her address was at an estate of expensive new houses just outside Yarmouth.

While Georgina filled in her details Helen helped the patient to take off her coat, then carried out routine observations, checking blood pressure, pulse and temperature.

'Can you tell us exactly what happened?' asked Helen when both she and Georgina had finished.

'I was approaching the precinct,' said the woman slowly. 'I had parked my car in the car park and I had taken a short cut through the park. It was while I was walking under the trees that I slipped on the path—I think the leaves were wet. Anyway, I put out my hand to save myself but the next thing I knew I was on the ground with a terrible pain in my wrist. I think I've broken it. I…I even heard a crack…it was awful.'

'You've also got a bump on your forehead,' said Georgina. 'Did you do that at the same time?'

'I don't know.' The woman put up her hand and touched her forehead in a bemused fashion. 'I suppose I must have done…'

'Does it hurt anywhere else?' asked Helen.

'My side hurts a bit, but that's probably just where I hit the ground. I felt so silly—there were a lot of shoppers in the precinct.'

'Never mind,' said Helen briskly. 'We'll just get the doctor to have a look at you, then I expect he'll want you to have an X-ray.' She glanced up as the curtain was opened an inch or two.

'May I come in?' said an all too recognisable voice from outside.

'Of course, Dr Sawyer,' said Helen. 'This is Eileen Clayton—she's had rather a bad fall and thinks she may have fractured her wrist.'

'Shall we take a look?' Nick came right into the cubicle and smiled down at the woman. Immediately she looked a little brighter. 'Now—is it *Mrs* Clayton?' he added as he examined her wrist.

The woman nodded in reply.

'Yes,' said Nick after a moment, 'it does look like a nasty break there, I'm afraid. We'll have some X-rays, please, Sister. And what about this lump?' Reaching out, he gently touched the lump on Mrs Clayton's forehead. 'You may have a bit of a headache or even a touch of concussion—that lump is growing by the minute.'

He smiled, that devastating smile guaranteed to charm the very birds out of the trees, thought Helen grimly.

'Are there any other injuries, Sister?' he asked, glancing up at Helen.

'Mrs Clayton mentioned that her side was painful.'

'In that case we'd better take a look at that as well,' said Nick.

'I'll go and organise an X-ray,' said Georgina.

Helen watched while Nick examined Mrs Clayton's side, hip and thigh.

'I don't think,' he said at last, straightening up, 'that there's anything broken there. But I would imagine there will be quite a bit of bruising when you wake up tomorrow morning.'

'Oh, dear.' Mrs Clayton pulled a face. 'I'm due to go on holiday in a couple of days.'

'There's no reason why you shouldn't still go,' said Nick. 'Where are you going?'

'Barbados.'

'Very nice.' He raised his eyebrows. 'You'll just have to make sure your husband does all the carrying of the cases because that wrist will probably be in plaster.'

'I don't have a husband, Doctor,' said Eileen Clayton. 'I'm divorced. And it wasn't my wrist I was worried about but the bruising...because it'll show when I'm wearing my bikini.'

Helen felt herself stiffen. The look on Eileen Clayton's face was reminiscent of the way that Anne Longman had gazed at Nick when she had first met him.

'She was all over him,' said Georgina a little later when she and Helen were alone again. 'Mind you, you could hardly blame her. He really is very dishy.'

'She wouldn't have got far,' said Helen unthinkingly. 'He doesn't like predatory females.'

'Really?' said Georgina with an amused glance. 'And how do you know that?'

'I just do, that's all.' Helen answered quickly, but she felt the colour touch her cheeks. 'I guess I heard him mention the fact at some time or another…'

'Well,' said Georgina, 'that may be so, but I shouldn't imagine it'll be too long before he gets snapped up by someone—not with those looks—you mark my words. It might not be an Eileen Clayton—far more likely to be one of the younger nurses.'

Helen remained silent. For some reason she found herself incapable of commenting on what Georgina had just said because she knew it to be true. Nick was very good-looking and it was probably only a matter of time before some beautiful young girl snapped him up—and there was no shortage of those amongst members of staff. What was really worrying was why the prospect should bother her so much and why, as the day went on, she should feel increasingly miserable whenever she thought about it.

CHAPTER NINE

IT WAS after dusk when Helen and Nick reached Fleetwood House and the huge bonfire had already been lit, its glow illuminating the paddock to one side of the house while the sweet aroma of applewood smoke filled the stillness of the November evening.

There were several other cars on the drive and as Helen drew to a halt they paused for a moment and gazed up at the front of the house which was lit by lights concealed in the shrubbery. It was a large Georgian-style house, pink-washed with two rows of symmetrical windows on either side of the imposing front entrance. 'The views in daylight across the Solent are magnificent,' said Helen as they climbed out of the car and walked round the house.

A large group of people were already congregated on the terrace. Children ran about in the gardens, their faces alight with excitement in the glow from the fire.

'Helen, Nick—hello.' Richard, his face smudged with black, greeted them. 'Help yourselves to a drink.' He waved towards a large table which had been set up on the terrace and was packed with bottles and cans. 'The food is still cooking,' he added. 'It should be ready soon.'

Country-and-western music drifted through the open French windows from Richard's hi-fi unit, and a delicious smell of food wafted across the terrace from the barbeque.

Nick poured drinks for himself and Helen, and someone called out to them in greeting. Jon and Kate were already there, and crossed the terrace to join them. Helen glimpsed Georgina and Andrew on the lawn with their two daughters, Lauren and Natasha. They seemed to have joined forces with the other partner at the Fleetwood Centre, Martin Hogan, and his wife, Patsy, and their children.

They were quickly drawn into the party atmosphere, which proved to be highly infectious, and as she sipped her wine Helen at last felt herself begin to relax. It was only then that she realised just how uptight she had allowed herself to become.

'Helen, how are you?' Quite suddenly Kate was by her side. 'It seems ages since we've had a chat.'

'Well, if you will do things like get married and flit off on honeymoon what can you expect?' Helen smiled at her friend.

'It was only a weekend,' protested Kate with a laugh. 'And what about you?'

'What about me?' Helen raised her eyebrows.

'Gallivanting off to London.'

'Hardly gallivanting,' she said. 'It was work.'

'Oh, really?' said Kate. She said it casually, innocently, but Helen found herself throwing her friend a sharp glance. It was almost as if she knew what had happened in London. But she couldn't possibly know...not unless Nick had said anything and, surely, he wouldn't have done that. Would he?

She turned her head slightly and looked across the terrace to where he stood, talking to Elizabeth French, the practice manager at the Fleetwood Centre, and her husband, Geoff.

Almost as if he'd sensed her, watching him, he turned to look at her. Their gazes met and it was as if some message passed between them, some profound under-standing, and for the briefest and strangest of moments it was as if there was no one else present—that she and Nick were alone in the crowd.

Then the moment was over and Helen realised that Kate had spoken again and she hadn't heard a word of what she'd said.

'Sorry, Kate.' She shook her head slightly. 'What did you say?' She turned to her friend again, dragging her gaze away from Nick, but as she did so she was only too aware from the slightly bemused expression on Kate's face that she had seen the look that had passed between herself and Nick.

The incident was forgotten as Richard suddenly an-nounced from the terrace that the firework display was about to begin. There were squeals of excitement from the children as the outside lighting was switched off. After one huge bang signalled the start of the show, and to an accompaniment of some cleverly chosen pieces of orchestral music, the night sky was filled with the scream of rockets followed by huge bursts of coloured stars.

As well as the aerial displays there were set pieces— dozens of Catherine wheels spinning in the darkness to-gether with shrieking, deafening firecrackers. Each ar-rangement seemed to outdo the previous one, encour-aging more and more appreciation from the gathered throng who oohed and aahed in time-honoured tradition.

When the final rockets pierced the sky and exploded in a burst of a million golden stars, the caterers whom Richard had employed began to distribute hot potatoes, dripping with melted cheese, roasted chestnuts and hot dogs packed with onions and oozing with tomato sauce.

'Helen.' Richard caught her eye as she stood along-side Kate, Nick and Jon on the terrace. 'Would you

change the music for me, please? I think Handel's
"Zadok the Priest" may be rather a heavy accompaniment for jacket potatoes. You know where everything
is, don't you?'

'Yes,' she replied, with a laugh. 'Of course.' Excusing
herself from the others, she hurried across the terrace
and through the French windows into the house. She
selected a more appropriate CD to accompany supper
and was just exchanging it with the one that was in the
player when she heard a slight sound beside her. She
looked over her shoulder and found that Nick had followed her into the room. She was about to speak, to say
something on the lines that maybe he should have stayed
outside, when she realised he was staring at the wall
above the mantelpiece.

'Is that her?' he said at last.

She didn't have to turn, knowing what was there, but
she did, slowly, until she was facing the huge portrait
that dominated the entire wall. Dark, almond-shaped
eyes laughed down at them from a face with a flawless
complexion, a mouth that was a little too wide and thick
black hair cut into a fringe and parted in the centre.

'Yes,' Helen said quietly, 'that's her. That's Diana.'

'She was a striking woman,' said Nick, still gazing at
the portrait.

'She was beautiful,' said Helen simply.

'Richard obviously intends that picture to remain
there,' Nick said.

'I would imagine so.' Turning, Helen scanned the
room and added, 'And the ones on the piano, and the
window-sill…'

'It's a bit like a shrine,' said Nick sharply, drawing in
his breath as he gazed around.

'You should see her bedroom,' said Helen. 'Everything is just as it was, just as she left it.'

'But why?' Nick turned to look at her.

She shrugged. 'He adored her,' she said simply.

'Well, yes, quite. I gathered that. But she's dead, for heaven's sake. It's commendable to remember her, but all this...' He waved one hand. 'It's a bit extreme, you must admit. And it can't be good for his children— they'll become locked in some sort of time warp at this rate.'

'Actually, they are surprisingly well adjusted,' said Helen.

'But you—what about you?' Nick was staring at her now.

'What about me?' she said lightly.

'It can't be a bundle of fun for you, being constantly reminded of his late wife at every tiff and turn,' he said gently.

'I told you, she was also a friend of mine,' said Helen with a helpless shrug.

'Even so, I would say that was pushing friendship to its absolute limits,' said Nick incredulously.

Helen shrugged again. She had become so used to the way things were at Fleetwood House that she hadn't thought to question it but, hearing Nick talk, she came to the conclusion that the whole thing might appear a little bizarre in the eyes of a stranger.

'You said before that Richard doesn't want to give up this house, didn't you?' Nick went on.

'Richard would never leave Fleetwood House,' she said. 'I've always known that. It's not only because it was Diana's home—it is also his family home, you see.'

'Hmm.' Nick sounded far from convinced.

Helen followed him back onto the terrace, passing

Martin Hogan on his way in. Martin had his usual harassed expression.

'Pager,' he muttered, half to Helen and Nick and half to himself. 'Where's the phone?'

'In the hall,' said Helen. 'Are you on call, Martin?'

'Someone has to be,' he muttered gloomily.

As they stepped outside Kate came across to Helen while Jon engaged Nick in conversation. 'Are you all right, Helen?' Kate asked with a frown.

'Yes,' said Helen sharply. 'I'm fine. Absolutely fine. Why?'

'I just wondered, that's all. You looked a bit strained there for a moment when you came out of the house, and I was just talking to Georgina and she seems concerned about you as well. You don't seem to have been quite yourself just lately.'

'Honestly!' Helen began. 'I wish everyone would—' That was as far as she got for at that moment Martin almost erupted onto the terrace.

'There's a major alert going out,' he said in a loud voice. Those nearest swung around to listen and as he began to speak others called for quiet. Gradually the chatter and laughter died away.

'What is it?' called Richard.

'Is it a fire?' said someone else.

'It's an incident at sea,' said Martin, and there were murmurings of surprise among the crowd. 'I don't know any further details,' he went on, 'but something has happened off Cowes and they are asking all medical staff to stand by. Sounds like there could be many casualties.'

They were mostly silent on the drive into Shalbrooke. Nick had offered to take the wheel and Helen had been content to let him, knowing that his driving would probably be faster than hers.

Some of the doctors, including Jon and Martin, went straight to Cowes to receive casualties while others, together with other medical staff, had joined the convoy of cars that wound its way through the narrow country lanes to the hospital.

Kate had stayed on call for the Fleetwood Centre and Richard said he would report to the theatre at the Shalbrooke when he had supervised the clearing up of the bonfire and the fireworks.

By the time Helen, Nick and the others arrived at the A and E unit the night staff were receiving the first reports of what had happened.

'Seems like it was some sort of collision,' said Mike Barber, the senior charge nurse. 'A chartered pleasure boat with a disco party on board had apparently moored in the Solent to watch a firework display on shore—first reports suggest it was struck by a container vessel.'

'Oh, God, how dreadful!' Helen hurried to her office. 'What news of casualties?'

'Well, two of our lifeboats are at the scene as well as rescue helicopters from the mainland, but the operation is being hampered by the darkness. First reports indicate there are several fatalities.'

The waiting was fraught with apprehension and while for Helen this was nothing new, so used was she to these life and death situations, even she found herself filled with a sense of dread and foreboding. Nick picked up on this and mentioned it as they waited.

'It's because we are such a small, close community,' she replied, in answer to his question. 'When something like this happens it's practically inevitable that we will know some of the casualties. The staff always get very tense. I remember once after a particularly bad motor-bike accident the pillion rider turned out to be the son of one of our staff nurses. It was awful.'

'Was he dead?' asked Nick.

'He died on the operating table,' said Helen with a little shudder as she recalled that particular night.

At that moment their attention was diverted by Elliot who, although not on duty, had heard the news on the local radio and had headed straight for the hospital. 'I thought you could probably do with every pair of hands you can get,' he said to Mike Barber.

'You're right there,' said Mike. 'We were just saying how quiet it had been, with only a couple of minor fire-work burns to deal with, and then this has to happen. Jon Hammond has just phoned in—he's down at Cowes on the seafront. It seems the boat has sunk.'

Helen stared at him, aghast. 'How many have they rescued, for heaven's sake?'

'There's no telling yet. Some people escaped on the boat's inflatable life rafts, others have been picked up by the Yarmouth lifeboat. Some, apparently, tried to swim for the shore. Ambulances are on their way in now. Oh, just a moment, there's a call coming through now from Control—' He broke off to take the call, and they all waited in an agony of suspense.

At last he replaced the handset and looked up. By this time everyone was gathered round the nurses' station, awaiting instructions. Already the red alert procedures had been put into operation, with extra medical supplies and blankets brought from the stores and the blood bank put on standby.

'Estimated time of arrival for the first two ambulances is five minutes,' said Mike. 'Survivors mostly suffering from shock, hypothermia and exposure. That water is very cold at this time of the year. Oh, and one other thing, I warn you—it's practically all young people—teenagers.'

One of the nurses came through from Reception at that moment. 'Mike, relatives are beginning to arrive. Where shall I ask them to wait? Oh, and the police are here as well, and a reporter from the local paper.'

'I'll sort all that out,' said Elliot, and he headed for Reception.

The medical staff began to move outside in readiness to receive the first of the survivors. There was a chill in the air, together with the pungent smell of bonfires, and there was stillness, a quietness that reminded Helen of the calm before a storm.

'Are you OK?' murmured Nick, who was standing just behind her.

'Yes.' She nodded, then gave a little sigh. Suddenly it was comforting to have him there with her, and in spite of the seriousness of the occasion she felt a sudden charge of adrenalin at his nearness.

It was then, in the stillness, that the gathered throng of medics heard the first distant wailing of a siren. Heads were raised, faces expectant and strangely ghostly in the eerie, yellow overhead lighting.

'Here we go,' said Nick. Unexpectedly he reached for Helen's hand, and under the cover of his white coat he squeezed it comfortingly just as the first of the ambulances, its blue lights flashing, drove into the hospital grounds.

The medical team swung into action its well-rehearsed red alert routine as the first of the survivors were taken from the ambulances and whisked away on trolleys into the treatment rooms.

Helen quickly became caught up in the drama and

tension as each of the young survivors was assessed and treated. Most were suffering from the effects of hypothermia, after being in the cold water. The paramedics and the medical staff at the scene of the incident had wrapped each victim in large space blankets in an effort to start the process of raising the body temperature.

As each patient was assessed, body temperature was recorded by a special low-reading rectal thermometer. A reading below 35°C was classed as subnormal and care had to be taken when reheating the body. This process had to be undertaken very slowly in case of shock, unless a reading below 33° was recorded, in which case the patient would require rapid warming in an intensive care unit as cardiac arrest and coma could follow.

Afterwards, when it was all over, the images sometimes crept into Helen's mind, haunting her for weeks— white faces with a bluish tinge, eyes staring with shock, teeth chattering with cold, wet hair matted with seaweed and salt. Young people, some little more than children, whose enjoyment had been so cruelly cut short, whose eyes had witnessed scenes they shouldn't have had to see; friends torn away from them and sinking beneath the waves, whose ears would until their dying day hear those screams of terror.

There were also other injuries, apart from the effects of shock and exposure—broken limbs that had to be X-rayed then set, heads gashed and bleeding, other wounds requiring sutures, one girl who had lost most of her teeth and another who was so hysterical it took herself, Nick and another nurse to hold her down to sedate her. There was a boy who for one mind-numbing moment she thought was Richard's son, Alex, until she remembered he had been with them all at Fleetwood House—could that really have only been that evening?

There were those for whom it was all too late, who had drowned, who had to be certified dead on arrival and who were then moved to the hospital chapel for identification purposes. And the relatives, the anguish on the faces of a seemingly never-ending stream of parents, grandparents, brothers, sisters and friends, all of them desperate, all searching, clinging to that last hope that the face they wanted to see above all others would be there to greet them—safe.

There were other images as well, things that as they happened might have been of little significance but which Helen recalled later: Nick, as he worked desperately to resuscitate a young girl and his subsequent anguish when he lost her; a young policeman so traumatised that he was incapable of telling a man and woman that their son was among the drowned and, of course, the dreadful inevitability when it happened; the nurse whose brother was amongst the injured and who subsequently herself had to be treated for shock.

There was the press to deal with. An over-enthusiastic reporter had to be firmly escorted from the premises, along with her photographer. Finally, there was the seemingly endless stream of enquiries from members of the public, all desperate for information.

Help arrived from many sources. The hospital chaplain was joined by local clergy, ministers from the Anglican and Methodist churches, a Catholic priest, and some from other faiths who all helped to counsel the shocked and bereaved.

Some casualties had to be taken elsewhere when the Shalbrooke was full—some to another Island hospital and others, those requiring specific treatment that was unavailable, were airlifted by helicopter to Southampton or Portsmouth.

Once, briefly, Helen was aware of a sense of relief when a tired, white-faced Dave Morey on his umpteenth trip to the hospital told her that Siobhan wasn't on duty that night. 'She wanted to come in,' he said, 'but I forbade her.'

'Quite right, too, Dave,' she said. 'You have another life to think about now.' And even in the midst of all the trauma and mayhem she was aware of another pang of something close to envy as she thought of Siobhan and that tiny foetus growing safely inside her.

But throughout it all—the drama and the anguish of that long night, the tension and the weariness—she was aware of one factor that overrode all others, and that was that Nick was there, working alongside her. Somehow it felt so right. Because he was there Helen felt able to face and deal with anything, terrible as some of it was. Together they worked—assessing, fighting when all seemed lost, administering, soothing, calming and comforting.

They sat in the staffroom in the cold grey light of the November dawn and took stock of the terrible toll of the night's disaster.

'At least twelve drowned,' said someone, 'and several still missing.'

'Everyone will know someone,' said Helen with a shiver as she curled her hands round a mug of steaming tea, drawing comfort from its warmth.

'There will be an extensive inquiry,' said someone else.

'Whose fault do you think it was?' asked one young nurse, her face etched with fatigue, so exhausted she could barely stay awake.

'I wouldn't even hazard a guess,' said Elliot wearily.

'Only an inquiry can deduce that. It could be that the pleasure boat was where it shouldn't have been or it may turn out to be the fault of the captain of the container vessel—who knows?' He looked around at the assembled staff. 'Whatever the outcome, our task is over. Thank you all for your excellent work. It's been a tough night. I suggest you go home now and get some rest.'

'Some of us should be on duty this morning,' said one nurse.

'I've covered you all with staff from the nursing bank,' said Elliot amidst sighs of relief.

Helen allowed Nick to drive them home to Gatcombe. Pale sunshine was struggling to penetrate an early morning mist and, really, it was just like any other November morning, so normal that it was hard to believe the horrors of the previous night and the shock that was still to greet many of the Island inhabitants as they awoke and heard the news.

Helen was too tired to think, let alone talk, and when Nick drove up the lane and onto the forecourt of the Coach House and switched off the engine neither of them made any attempt to get out of the car. As if it was the most natural thing in the world, she rested her head on his shoulder.

They were silent for a long while, content simply to sit there. In the end it was Nick who broke the silence. 'It's been quite a night,' he said softly.

'Yes,' Helen sighed. 'And there will be a lot of devastated people in its aftermath.'

They fell silent again, each reflecting on their own thoughts and the images that filled their minds, then Helen said, 'I want to go to bed, but I am so tired I'm not sure I can even get out of the car.' As she spoke she turned her face, lifting it slightly. The next moment Nick covered her lips with his own in a kiss exquisitely tender and gentle.

She knew she should stop him, but she had neither the strength nor the inclination. And what did it matter? What did any of it matter? What was a kiss, after all, in the face of such appalling tragedy?

At last he drew back and she felt vaguely bereft. She had wanted the moment to last for ever, just her and Nick in the silence and solitude of the car with nothing else required of them—no one to make any demands on them, no decisions to be made and, above all, no recriminations.

At that moment from deep inside the house they both heard the sound of a single bark, a reminder that the outside world still existed.

'Poor old Chester will be crossing his legs by now,' said Nick.

Helen managed a weak smile. 'Yes,' she said with a sigh. 'I must go and let him out.' She turned to get out of the car then stopped as she felt Nick's hand on her arm.

'Helen,' he said softly.

'No, Nick,' she replied. 'Not now.'

'We have to, you know,' he said gently. 'We have to talk about it some time. I don't think it's just going to go away on its own.'

'I know,' she said with another sigh. 'But not now.'

CHAPTER TEN

IT WAS Sunday morning. Helen lay in bed, listening to the peal of church bells drifting across the fields from nearby Carisbrooke and watching the sunlight form patterns on the misty blue wallpaper as she wondered how she would spend her day. Usually she went to Fleetwood House on a Sunday, where she joined Richard, his children, his parents and Diana's mother for lunch. Usually she was quite happy to do so, even looked forward to it, so why this morning did she feel so restless?

She'd done very little the previous day, having spent most of the morning catching up on some sleep after the traumas of the previous night then doing a little housework and gardening. And she'd been quite content with that. It was only now, with time on her hands, that she felt strangely restless.

She slipped out of bed, crossed to the window and drew back the curtains, her gaze immediately drawn to the stable block. The door to the flat was shut, although Nick's curtains were open. He'd gone into work for a time the day before and, to her dismay, Helen had found herself wondering when he would be back. He still hadn't returned when she'd finally gone to bed and she'd lain there in the darkness, listening for his return and wondering who he was with.

At last she'd heard the noise of a car in the lane, voices and then the slam of a car door, followed by the sound of footsteps crunching on the gravel drive.

Even then sleep had eluded her as she'd speculated

on the identity of his companion. Was it one of the nurses from work? Or maybe one of the secretarial staff? She obviously had a car, whoever she was, and she hadn't merely brought him home at the end of his shift because that would have ended hours ago. They must have gone for a drink somewhere, or maybe a meal— just like the meals she and Nick had shared in London. Torment had followed as her imagination had slipped into overdrive, ending with exasperation as she'd thumped her pillow and severely reprimanded herself.

She had to stop monitoring Nick's actions. It was absolutely no business of hers what he did or with whom. He'd said they still needed to talk but as far as Helen was concerned there was little to talk about. He'd said her relationship with Richard was flawed in some way. She'd thought and thought about that, but had always come to the conclusion that he was wrong. He hardly knew Richard and certainly knew nothing of their past so how could he be in a position to judge something like that?

She'd tried to make it plain to Nick that their relationship could go no further so she had to accept the inevitable fact that he would get on with the rest of his life. So why was she finding that so difficult?

She'd slept eventually, albeit fitfully, and now, on waking, she felt heavy-eyed and unrefreshed.

Slipping out of her room, she padded down the narrow passage to the bathroom with its white-panelled walls and dark green tiling. After a long soak in the huge Victorian bath she felt a little better, and was just climbing out when she heard the phone ringing in the bedroom. Wrapping herself in a fluffy white towel, she padded back to the bedroom, sat on her bed and lifted the receiver.

It was Kate. 'Helen,' she said. 'I hope I didn't get you out of bed.'

'No, of course not. I'd just got out of the bath, actually.'

'Sorry. You're not dripping everywhere, I hope?'

'No. Go on.'

'I was just wondering what you were doing today, that's all.'

'Well, I usually go to Fleetwood House…'

'Yes, I know that, but seeing that Richard is on call…'

'Is he? I hadn't realised that.' Her heart sank at the prospect of spending the day with Richard's parents and Diana's mother.

'Yes,' said Kate, 'he swopped with Martin. Martin and Patsy have to go to the mainland for some family celebration or something. But Jon is playing squash with Nick later this morning…'

'Oh, really?' said Helen. Her interest was aroused now.

'Yes, they arranged it last night. Nick came here for dinner.'

So that's where he had been. With Kate and Jon. Not on a date with one of the nurses. Quite suddenly she felt better.

'And I was wondering,' Kate went on, 'whether you would like to come over here with me. It's ages since we had a really good natter. Bring Chester. We could take him for a walk along the beach then the men could join us for lunch. What do you say?'

'I would love to, Kate,' she said, with no hesitation. The day was looking brighter by the minute. 'I'll ring Fleetwood House. I'm sure no one will mind if I wriggle out of lunch, especially if Richard isn't going to be around. What time would you like me to come over?'

'As soon as you like,' said Kate. 'Jon is picking Nick up around ten to go to the sports centre so you come over when you're ready.'

By the time she replaced the receiver she felt as if the day ahead was a completely different one from the one she'd visualised when she'd woken.

'So how's married life?' Helen threw Kate a sidelong glance as they strolled on the vast expanse of beach. The tide was out and in the end they had gone to Appley beach, away from the shingle at Cowes, so that Chester could have a good run. He foraged ahead of them now with his nose down and his tail in the air as he examined interesting smells around clumps of seaweed. They had already discussed the aftermath of Friday night's tragedy and Kate's subsequent involvement with the bereaved before their conversation had turned to personal matters.

'Wonderful,' said Kate. 'Absolutely wonderful. I fully recommend it. I only wish it had happened years ago— but with Jon, of course, not with Alistair.'

Helen shot her a quick glance. Alistair Cunningham had been the previous man in Kate's life but their relationship had ended rather abruptly about five years ago when Alistair had gone to the States to work and Kate had returned from her job in London to go into partnership at the Fleetwood Centre.

It had only been fairly recently that Kate had told Helen that Alistair had been killed in an accident some considerable time ago. She had often wondered why it had taken Kate so long to impart that particular piece of information, but shortly afterwards Kate had married Jon Hammond and the matter had seemed to lose its relevance. Now, with mention of Alistair again, her curiosity was aroused once more.

'I wish you'd told me earlier about Alistair's death,' she said. 'It must have been a terrible time for you and I would have liked to have been able to help you through it.'

'It happened a long time after we split up,' said Kate.

'Even so, it must still have been distressing.'

Kate was silent for a moment then, hunching her shoulders slightly and thrusting her hands into the pockets of her jacket, she said, 'Yes, I suppose it was, but not for the reasons you might think.'

'What do you mean?' Helen frowned.

'Well, it wasn't as distressing as the relationship itself,' replied Kate grimly. She spoke so quietly that just for one moment Helen thought she might have misheard her. She was about to ask her what she had said when Kate carried on talking. 'It wasn't what you thought, Helen,' she said. 'It wasn't what anyone thought. Alistair wasn't what anyone thought. The face he showed to the world was that of a charming, well-educated, respected lawyer. The face I saw was very different.'

'Whatever do you mean?' Helen looked at Kate, wondering what she might be about to hear.

'It was dreadful, Helen.' Kate's voice suddenly shook and when Helen looked at her she was concerned to see that her face looked white and pinched, as if even recalling the past was something of a strain. 'It was dreadful,' she repeated. 'I only just got out in time. If I'd stayed I doubt I would have survived…'

'My God, Kate,' said Helen utterly shocked now, 'are you saying he knocked you about?'

'That's probably an understatement.' Kate gave a short humourless laugh. 'But, yes, he beat me up on more than one occasion. He also raped me.' Her voice broke and, obviously fighting tears, she turned her head and stared out to sea.

Helen stared at her friend in dismay, hardly able to believe what she had just heard. 'I wish you'd said,' she whispered at last, her hand on Kate's arm. 'Oh, if only you'd said.'

'I couldn't tell you,' said Kate. 'I didn't want anyone to know.'

'Are you saying no one knows?' asked Helen.

'Only Jon,' said Kate quietly.

'Jon? You told Jon?'

Kate nodded. 'Jon helped me to face it,' she said. 'He was wonderful…is wonderful. He is so gentle, so tender. He showed me how to put it all behind me—to live again, to trust again and, above all, to love again.'

They walked on in silence for a time, with Helen coming to terms with what Kate had just revealed. It had answered a lot of questions, mainly fears that Jon had confided to her when he had been getting to know Kate, fears that Kate seemed nervous maybe even frigid— ideas which at the time had seemed alien to Helen and which later she had put down to delayed shock over Alistair's death. Now it seemed the truth had been very different, and it had taken Kate's husband to bring about the healing process.

At last Helen spoke again. 'Do you and Jon have any plans to start a family?' she asked, secure enough in her friendship with Kate to know that she could ask such a question.

'We're not sure,' Kate replied. 'At first I thought probably not…but now, well, I don't know… It completes something somehow… But, if we are, we shall have to get on with it soon.' She laughed and her expression lightened, easing the strain of earlier. 'No hanging about. Not at our age.'

Helen smiled. 'No,' she said, 'I suppose not. It doesn't matter when you're Siobhan's age but, having said that, one can't exactly accuse them of hanging about. I suppose you know about that, being Siobhan's GP?'

Kate nodded. 'Yes, Siobhan's been to see me. She's over the moon and so, I gather, is Dave.'

'I know. It even made me feel broody,' said Helen ruefully. 'But in my case that syndrome would need to be firmly suppressed.'

'I don't see why,' said Kate. 'A lot of women are having first babies in their late thirties these days, women who've put their careers first—or who've had other commitments.'

'Yes, I know,' said Helen. 'But I guess it would make more sense to be married first. Oh, I know there are plenty who don't, but that wouldn't do for me. I've always been of the opinion that a baby needs two parents around.'

'Yes, quite.' Kate paused and they carried on walking, their trainers leaving a trail of imprints in the wet sand. Then hesitantly she threw Helen a glance. 'Any update on the marriage scene for you?' she asked.

Helen shook her head. 'Not really,' she said with a shrug.

'I thought after your dad died...' Kate trailed off, the question left hanging in the air.

'I dare say it'll happen one day,' said Helen. 'I've waited this long so I don't suppose a few more months...or even years...will make much difference.' She was aware that a dull, flat note had entered her voice but she seemed unable to do anything about it.

They walked on in silence for a while. Helen kept

throwing a piece of driftwood for Chester and time and again he brought it back to drop it at their feet, his tail waving ecstatically as he ran alongside them waiting for it to be thrown again.

'Helen?' said Kate at last.

'Yes?' Helen swallowed, anticipating what was coming.

'Is everything all right between you and Richard?'

'Yes, fine,' she said quickly. 'Why shouldn't it be?'

'I don't know, really.' Kate shrugged. 'Just a feeling I've had, I suppose. Don't forget I've known you both for a very long time.'

'You also know I've loved Richard for a very long time,' said Helen.

'I know that you loved Richard before he married Diana,' said Kate, and she seemed to be choosing her words with extreme care. 'What happened after Diana died I'm not really sure. Whether you'd simply put your feelings for Richard on hold during his marriage and revived them later, or whether you fell in love with him all over again, I don't know.'

'Does it matter?' asked Helen. She knew the same dull note was still in her voice.

'Yes,' said Kate, 'actually, I think it does. Because if you haven't fallen in love with him again I would question whether it's right to even consider marrying him.'

'And if my feelings had been put on hold?'

'Again, I would question them.'

'What you're saying is that he preferred Diana to me, isn't it?'

Kate looked uncomfortable.

'Go on,' said Helen with a short laugh, 'admit it.'

'Well, yes, to put it bluntly, I suppose that is what I do mean.'

'Second best, you mean?' There was a bitter note in Helen's voice, and Kate threw her a quick, concerned glance.

'Helen, I'm sorry,' she said helplessly.

Helen shrugged. 'Don't worry, I don't suppose you are the first one to have thought it. Anyway, it doesn't matter because it isn't like that. I know it isn't, and Richard knows it isn't. We are very fond of one another.'

'I'm sure you are, Helen, and as long as he loves you and you love him then, really, nothing else matters.' Kate paused. 'If, on the other hand,' she went on after a moment, 'you doubted that love, even for a moment, then it would be wrong to go on, and certainly wrong to marry.'

They walked on again, without speaking, the only sounds around them those of the cries of gulls as they swooped and dived overhead, the sound of a ship's horn far out on the horizon and the occasional bark of excitement from Chester as he raced across the sand.

'You do still love him, don't you?' Kate half turned to her as she spoke and for the moment Helen found herself unable to answer, her throat suddenly tight with tears.

'Helen, what is it?' Kate's hand was on her arm and it was almost Helen's undoing. Still powerless to speak, Helen simply shook her head.

'There's someone else, isn't there?' Kate's voice was soft now.

Angrily Helen dashed away her tears with the back of her hand as they suddenly spilled over and trickled down her cheeks. 'It'll go away.' At last she managed to speak. 'It has to go away. It isn't fair to Richard.'

'And if it doesn't go away? Would that be fair to Richard? A lifetime of pretence?' said Kate gently.

'Come to that, would it be fair to you, living a lie? Or to Nick?'

Helen stopped dead and stared at Kate. 'You know,' she said at last. When Kate nodded ruefully she added, 'Oh God, am I that transparent? How many other people know?'

'It's different for me,' said Kate. 'Like I said, I know you very well. I think Georgina may have guessed, but I doubt if anyone else has.'

'What am I going to do?' Hopelessly Helen stared at Kate.

'You are in love with Nick?'

'I don't know. I'm not sure. I've never felt this way before so how can I tell?'

'Not even with Richard the first time around?'

'Not even with Richard. I thought that was love at the time. Now I wonder if it wasn't simply a schoolgirl crush, or infatuation, or something. There have been one or two relationships since that didn't really amount to much and then Richard again but, honestly, Kate, I've never felt this way before.'

'Want to talk about it?' asked Kate. 'Seeing this is turning into girls' confession time.'

Helen threw her a glance and suddenly she realised that she did want to talk, probably partly because Kate was a doctor and well used to dealing with situations of this kind, but even more than that because she was a friend and understood her. 'Yes,' she said, 'I think I have to, otherwise I fear I might go mad.'

She hesitated for a long moment, trying to collect her thoughts, while Kate remained silent then she said, 'Did you know Nick was at that conference I went to in London?'

Kate nodded. 'Yes,' she said. 'He did mention that he was there.'

'I was pleased to see him,' Helen went on, after she'd recovered from the fact that Nick had told Kate—and probably Jon as well—that he had been at the conference. 'Because...well, you know how it is at these things. It's just nice to see someone you know...'

'Not because you fancied him?'

'Of course not!'

'Not just a little teeny bit?' said Kate. 'Not when you first met him at the wedding? He is very attractive, after all, very good-looking—you have to admit that.'

'Well, yes, yes, he is,' said Helen. 'Oh, all right, I admit it. I did find him attractive but—'

'And you knew he found you attractive?'

'Well...'

'Biggest aphrodisiac around, as far as I'm concerned.' Kate raised her eyebrows and Helen gave a sigh.

'OK,' she said. 'I admit it. Yes, I found him attractive and, yes, I knew he was attracted to me.'

'Right,' said Kate. 'So let's get this straight. There's the pair of you in a top London hotel, both single, both free and fancying each other like mad—go on.'

'Kate, for goodness' sake,' protested Helen, 'you're making it sound like some sort of orgy. It wasn't like that at all.'

'Oh, really?' said Kate innocently. 'So you didn't sleep with him, then?'

'I...I...'

'You did sleep with him? I was right the first time?'

'Kate, you are not making this easy for me. It really wasn't what you are implying.'

'I'm not implying anything,' Kate replied calmly. 'I'm quite simply trying to look dispassionately at the facts.

You two quite obviously got together and found you
wanted it to be much more than a one-night stand.'

'No—' Helen began.

'No?' Kate interrupted. 'I wouldn't have thought one-
night stands were your scene at all, Helen, and they quite
obviously aren't Nick's.'

'What do you mean?' Helen threw Kate a startled
glance, wondering what else Nick had told her.

'Well, if they were, if he was used to that sort of thing,
he would hardly have turned up here to work barely a
week later, would he?'

'But he'd applied for the job at the Shalbrooke before
then,' protested Helen. 'He told me that afterwards.'

'He could always have turned the job down when he
heard he'd got it,' said Kate bluntly. 'But he didn't. He
carried on and came here. Hardly the actions of a man
who had indulged in a one-night stand that he didn't
want repeated, you have to admit.'

'No...I suppose not.'

'So what did you think when he turned up at the
Shalbrooke?' asked Kate.

'I was horrified.'

Kate gave a short laugh. 'Yes, I dare say you were.
You thought your little indiscretion would be lost in
London's mists of time, along with millions of others,
didn't you? Instead of that, suddenly here he is on your
doorstep and it seemed your sins were about to find you
out. Interesting. What did you do?'

'I told him there was no chance we could continue
with...well, with anything.'

'And did he accept that?' Kate raised one sceptical
eyebrow.

'I thought he did...at first,' said Helen. 'But then almost before I knew what was happening he'd moved into the stable flat—and that was partly your fault, Kate!'

'Sorry.' Kate was laughing now.

'I'm glad you find all this so funny,' snapped Helen. Bending down, she picked up the piece of driftwood that Chester had just dropped yet again and hurled it as far as she could.

'I'm sorry,' Kate said again as Chester streaked ahead of them once more. 'Really, I am. But, you have to admit, Helen, it does have its comical side, you know.'

'I wish I could see it. All I can see at the moment is misery and heartbreak whichever way I look at it…and pain. Pain for Richard if I tell him I've met someone else—'

'And misery and heartbreak for you and Nick if you don't,' said Kate bluntly. This time there was no trace of humour in her voice. When Helen remained silent she said, 'Do you really think Richard would be as devastated as you fear?'

Helen gave a helpless shrug. 'I don't know,' she said. 'He's been through so much, what with losing Diana and everything. I just don't think I can put him through any more.'

'What does Nick think?'

'I think he imagines if he stays around for a while I might change my mind.' She paused. 'He also thinks there's something wrong with my relationship with Richard.'

'What does he mean?' Kate threw her a sideways glance.

'I'm not sure.' Helen admitted. 'He says it's something he's not able to put his finger on—some flaw, he said.'

'That's interesting,' said Kate. 'Very often an outsider will see something that the rest of us have failed to.'

'I think it's only because he wants there to be something wrong,' said Helen shortly.

'Maybe,' agreed Kate. 'But it must be nice to be pursued, to be wanted, especially by someone as dishy as Nick Sawyer. Go on, Helen, you can't deny that.'

'No.' Helen gave another sigh. 'I can't deny it.' Then she smiled. 'It is nice.'

'So, what was he like?' asked Kate curiously. 'Go on, tell. This is just us now. I won't tell another soul.'

'Not even Jon?'

'Not even Jon.'

'Cross your heart and hope to die?'

'Cross my heart and hope to die.' With a laugh Kate repeated the phrase from their schooldays.

'Absolutely fabulous,' said Helen with a sigh.

By the time Helen and Kate returned to Kate's waterfront apartment at Cowes the two men had returned from their game of squash and were sitting on the balcony, enjoying the warmth of the sudden unexpected autumn sunshine that had finally struggled through the mist.

'How did your game go?' asked Helen, looking from one to the other.

'I must be out of condition.' Jon looked up with a laugh. 'He thrashed me.'

Nick, who was lounging in a wicker chair with a baseball cap pulled down over his face, lifted the brim slightly and winked at Helen. Her heart turned over and hastily she followed Kate back into the apartment and through to the kitchen to help prepare lunch.

'It's so warm I think we could eat outside,' said Kate.

Together they carried salads, pâté, French bread, pasta

drenched in a sun-dried tomato sauce and red and white wine onto the balcony, where they found the men had roused themselves sufficiently to set the chairs around the wrought-iron table.

'Did you girls enjoy your walk?' asked Jon as he poured the wine.

'Oh, yes,' Kate replied. 'Very much. It was very—er—bracing. I think Chester is as shattered as you are, Jon.' As she spoke there came the sound of a loud snore from the sitting room where Chester was stretched out on the rug, periodically twitching with delight as in his dreams he still raced across the sands.

They all laughed and Jon raised his glass in a toast to friendship and they joined him. Helen sipped her wine and reflected that this precise moment, in the company of dear friends, with good food and wine, with sunshine sparkling on the sea before them and with the man she loved at her side, was the nearest thing to heaven she could have imagined.

It was with a little jolt a split second later that she came back to earth and realised that for the first time she had acknowledged something she had hitherto resisted, even to herself—the fact that she loved Nick. Talking to Kate had obviously helped her to clarify her emotions. Not that it changed anything. The situation remained the same.

With a sigh, she leaned back in her chair, lifted her face to the sun and allowed herself to relax and just for a while to indulge in this little taste of heaven which, after all, couldn't last.

And all too soon, of course, it was over. As all good things had to, with the cooling of the sun and the springing up of a breeze that blew in from the sea, it came to an end.

With sighs of regret the group moved to gather up the empty plates and glasses and return them to the kitchen. After they'd said their goodbyes, and with Chester—who by this time was raring to go once more—safely stowed in the back seat of Helen's car, she and Nick took their leave and headed once more for Gatcombe as dusk began to fall.

Still Helen refused to think, content to drift in that other world where everything was easy, where no difficult decisions had to be made and where no one was hurt by the actions of another.

She and Nick were mostly silent on the drive home, but it was that comfortable silence which is born of familiarity and the sense of well-being that comes from being with the right person.

When they reached the Coach House it seemed the most natural thing in the world, after the time they had just shared, for Nick to come indoors with her rather than take himself off to the solitude of his flat. And as the door closed behind them and he drew her into his arms it not only seemed natural but utterly inevitable.

They were interrupted half an hour later by the ringing of the telephone.

'Leave it,' groaned Nick from the depths of the sofa.

'I can't,' said Helen, sitting up, pushing back her hair and buttoning her shirt.

'It's for you,' she said a moment later, coming back into the room and handing him the cordless phone.

'Me?' He looked amazed. 'Is it the hospital?'

'No.' She shook her head. 'It's your mother.'

'My mother!' He sat bolt upright, his eyes widening in comical dismay. 'What in the world does she want?'

'You'd better find out.' Helen suppressed her laughter and left him to it, going out of the room and closing the door softly behind her.

CHAPTER ELEVEN

'IT SEEMS,' said Nick ten minutes later when he came to find Helen, 'that it's make-my-mind-up time.'

Helen, who had just given Chester his dinner, looked up quickly. 'In what way?' she said.

'Remember I told you about the practice founded by my late father?' said Nick as they watched Chester wolf down his food.

Helen smiled. 'And how your mother lives in hopes that you will go into the practice and carry it on?'

Nick pulled a face and nodded. 'I suppose I always knew that one day it would happen but I hadn't visualised it quite yet. My father's partner, Oliver, took on a junior partner a short while ago but now it seems Oliver has a heart problem. No doubt mindful of my father's untimely death, Oliver's wife has persuaded him to hang up his stethoscope.'

'Leaving junior partner on his own?' said Helen quietly. Already warning bells were sounding in her head. This was it. Nick would go back to Norfolk, sooner even than she had imagined, and most probably she would never see him again.

He nodded. 'Yes,' he said. 'Trouble is, junior partner is very young and does not have enough experience to be on his own. Apparently, they've all had a powwow up there and it was agreed that they would ask me first.'

'What if you refuse?'

'Two options—either they advertise for another partner or the practice merges with another in the area. But

157

they don't want that to happen because this other practice was always considered as a rival one, even though
in a very friendly sort of way.'

She swallowed. 'So what will you do?' She couldn't
bring herself to look at him. Instead she continued to
watch Chester, who had finished his meal and was moving his bowl around the floor as he licked it clean.

'I guess the time has come.' Nick sighed and pushed
back his hair. 'I always knew it would—I suppose I just
hadn't thought it would be yet, that's all. I had almost
promised myself one more stint abroad but—' He
shrugged, leaving the sentence unfinished.

'Where will you live? With your mother?' Helen
asked dully.

'Good Lord, no.' He looked faintly startled. 'I may
love my mother dearly but I couldn't live with her any
more, I suspect, than she could live with me. No, I shall
look for a suitable property in the area. There are some
beautiful old places around Norfolk that only require
time, money and a bit of imagination...'

An image of an old converted farmhouse in the
Norfolk countryside flitted through Helen's mind and
with a supreme effort was just as speedily dismissed.

'Besides...' Nick paused and looked down at her, then
put the phone down onto the table and put his hands on
her shoulders. 'I've always thought it a mistake to live
with in-laws, don't you?'

She stared at him, not understanding his meaning at
first. As it slowly dawned on her what he might be saying she realised that her heart had begun to beat very
fast. 'What do you mean?' she said at last, her voice
little more than a whisper.

'Marry me, Helen,' he said urgently. He drew her
close. 'Marry me, and come to Norfolk with me. Help

me find an old farmhouse that we can make a home for ourselves and our children.'

'But—'

'I love you,' he said, his voice suddenly husky with emotion. 'I've loved you from the moment I saw you at Kate's wedding. I want to make you my wife and I want you to be the mother of my children. But...' as she attempted to speak, to protest, he pressed his fingers against her lips '...I don't want you to answer me now. I want you to think about it—to go away and consider everything. At this moment you will probably tell me what I don't want to hear so don't say anything...please, Helen.'

Helplessly she continued to gaze up at him, her mind in turmoil, until at a sudden, single bark from Chester they both looked down. The dog was sitting, gazing expectantly up at the two of them. His ears and eyes were alert and his tail thumped the floor.

'He wants to know what would happen to him,' said Helen weakly.

'He would come with us, of course,' said Nick.

The weather changed dramatically following the Indian summer conditions of the weekend and gale force winds lashed the Wight, whipping up mountainous seas in the Channel and stripping the trees of the last of their autumn colours.

For the next few days Helen felt as if she herself was going through similar tumult as she walked a precarious tightrope between highest elation and bouts of deepest despair—elation from the knowledge that Nick really loved her, and despair from doubting whether she could do anything about it.

She wasn't sure how she managed to do her job, it

was as if she functioned on autopilot. She hoped no one noticed and maybe she would have got away with things if Georgina hadn't returned to the unit after a couple of days' leave.

It was the middle of the morning and Reception was packed. Helen had just come into the nurses' station from her office, where she had been dealing with a mountain of paperwork, Nick and Susan Joliffe were both in the treatment rooms, where the victims of two separate accidents were being treated, and Georgina was dealing with that morning's 'walking wounded'.

'Did you have a nice break?' asked Helen.

'Yes, lovely, thanks.' Georgina looked up from the list of patients' names that she had been studying. 'Andrew was off as well. The girls were at school and we spent the time decorating at the cottage and sorting out a few other odd jobs. It was bliss—we haven't done that sort of thing for a very long time.'

'No regrets about remarrying?' asked Helen softly.

'Absolutely not,' Georgina replied firmly. 'There's been some re-adjustment—of course there has—but I can't believe now that we wasted so much time.'

'I hope you're taking note of this,' said a voice suddenly from behind them.

Helen and Georgina both swung round to find that, unbeknown to them, Nick had come out of the treatment room and was standing there, well within earshot.

'Oh, Nick,' said Georgina, with a laugh. 'I didn't see you there. What do you mean—you hope Helen's taking note?'

'What I said,' said Nick solemnly. 'I overheard you, Georgina, say that you had no regrets about marrying Andrew again and that you couldn't believe you'd wasted so much time. I was simply hoping that Helen was taking note. Life is definitely too short to waste time. When you know you want something you have to go for it.'

'Absolutely,' said Georgina emphatically. Quickly she looked from Nick to Helen and then back again, as if she wasn't entirely sure what was going on but at the same time knew it was something important.

An awkward silence followed until Georgina said, 'Actually, I was having a similar sort of conversation with Dot last evening.'

'Dot?' Helen seized the opportunity to divert the conversation away from Nick and herself. 'How is she?'

'She's doing very well. She's over at Yarmouth, staying with Norman Westfield's sister while she gets over her operation.'

'Do you think there may be wedding bells there in the not too distant future?' asked Nick, and Helen recognised the wicked gleam in his eye as he manoeuvred the conversation back to his advantage again.

'It certainly seems possible,' said Georgina. 'At one time I wouldn't have thought so, but now, well, everything seems to have changed, doesn't it, Helen?' She turned to look at her. 'What with Dot's condition and everything.'

'Yes,' Helen agreed. 'It does.'

'You mean, it took that to make her realise what was right under her nose?' asked Nick innocently. 'Bit drastic, if you ask me.'

'Yes,' agreed Georgina, once more looking from Nick to Helen and back to Nick again, as if by now she was even more convinced that the conversation was loaded with innuendo and there was definitely something she was missing.

This was borne out a little later, during a lull in the

number of patients, when Georgina tracked Helen down in her office.

Helen's heart sank as she recognised the purposeful look on her friend's face as she came right into the room and shut the door firmly behind her. It had been bad enough at the weekend with Kate. Now it seemed she was to be interrogated yet again.

'So, what was all that about earlier on?' Sparing her nothing, Georgina came right to the point.

'I don't know what you're talking about.' Helen played for time.

'Yes, you do,' said Georgina bluntly. 'You know exactly what I'm talking about and I want to know.'

Helen gave a helpless shrug and, picking up a folder from the desk, made a show of sorting through a set of patient's records.

'What was Nick going on about? All that about life being too short, not wasting time and going for what you want?' When Helen remained silent Georgina went on, 'Is he in love with you, Helen?'

Helen became very still. She knew, however, that she couldn't hope to fool Georgina any more than she could fool Kate. While she and Kate knew each other so well from years of friendship, she and Georgina had an understanding of each other that came from many years of being not only friends but colleagues. At last she sighed and said, 'I suppose he must be if he's asked me to marry him.'

The silence in the small room was so profound that for a moment it was as if the world beyond ceased to exist.

Georgina could have reacted with shock, amazement or a cry of delight, but she did none of these. Instead, she simply stared at Helen then stepped forward and gave her a hug that adequately summed up her quiet pleasure.

'I'm so pleased,' she whispered at last. 'So very, very pleased.'

'I haven't agreed yet,' said Helen, her voice low.

'But you will,' said Georgina, her voice full of certainty. 'You will because you are in love with him. You've been in love with him from the very start, haven't you?'

Helen nodded. 'Yes,' she said helplessly. 'I suppose I have. But…but… Oh, Georgina, if only it were that simple.'

'But it *is* that simple,' said Georgina, her eyes shining. 'You love him and he loves you—nothing could be simpler.' She paused and threw Helen a searching glance. 'Is it Richard you're worried about?' she said.

'Yes,' said Helen weakly. 'I suppose it is. I'm not sure I can be that cruel.'

'You're absolutely right. You certainly can't be that cruel,' said Georgina firmly. 'To my mind, one of the worst things that someone can do is to marry one person when they are in love with another.'

Helen stared at her. 'So what do I do, Georgie? For God's sake, tell me, what do I do?'

'You tell him,' she replied. 'You go to Richard straight away and you tell him what has happened.'

She continued to stare at Georgina, knowing in her heart that what her friend said was right but uncertain she had the courage to do it. She almost welcomed the sound of the telephone that suddenly disturbed the highly charged atmosphere. She grabbed the receiver.

It was Elliot, demanding to know where all his staff were.

'We're with you, Elliot,' said Helen in relief. 'Sorry, we'll be right there.'

'We have a child screaming its head off because his fingers are stuck in some kitchen appliance, a teenager who's taken an overdose and needs a stomach wash-out and an elderly lady who's had a fall down a flight of stairs. And if all that isn't enough—' Elliot sounded really irritable now '—there's yet another RTA on its way in.'

'Some things never change.' Helen pulled a face as she replaced the receiver.

The two of them made their way back to the noise and bustle of Reception. The screams of the toddler still filled the air, a young man with his hand wrapped in a towel was dripping a trail of blood all over the floor and in one corner a girl was being sick in a wastebin.

'I'll see if I can help with that child,' said Helen, making her way in the direction of the screams, while Georgina began to question the young man with the cut hand who by this time beginning to look very pale.

The screams grew even louder as Helen approached the cubicle, and when she drew back the curtain she found the child, a little boy of about two, sitting on the bed. His face was brick-red and his blond hair stuck up in damp spikes all over his head. He was accompanied by a young woman, presumably his mother, who was anxiously watching as Nick tried to extricate the boy's hand from what looked like a blue plastic ball.

'Hello, young man,' said Helen. 'Whatever have you been up to?'

The toddler stopped screaming but only for the space of time it took for him to establish that someone else had arrived and to fill his lungs again for a fresh on-slaught.

'He's got his hand stuck,' said the young woman un-necessarily.

'What is it stuck in?' asked Helen, leaning forward for a better look.

'It's the ball that the washing liquid goes in,' said the woman. 'He took it out of the washing machine when I opened the door and put his fingers inside, then we couldn't get them out.'

'What are you using, Nick?' asked Helen above the child's screams.

'Vaseline,' said Nick. 'Could you try and distract him, Helen?'

'Sure.' Helen smiled and took Nick's stethoscope from the pocket of his white coat, dangling it in front of the little boy's face. At first he took no notice at all. If anything, his screams grew even louder and more frantic. When Helen tried to put it round his own neck he quite simply didn't want to know and struggled even more, making it practically impossible for Nick to work on his hand.

And then, quite suddenly—almost as if someone had flicked a switch—his screams stopped, subsiding into hiccups as he discovered Helen's fob watch pinned to the front of her uniform.

He stared, blinked and reached out with his other hand to investigate more fully. Helen moved closer and put her arms loosely around him as chubby little fingers stabbed, probed and then closed over the watch, tugging and twisting.

Moments later there came a grunt of satisfaction from Nick as the ball slid off the child's hand. By this time the toddler's fascination with Helen's fob watch was to-tal and the parting from the plastic ball, until then a matter of prime importance, paled into insignificance.

'There's no great harm done,' Nick explained to the boy's relieved mother. 'The skin is red and a little grazed in places and there will probably be some bruising, but his fingers are fine—no breaks. Even the ball is still in one piece. Mind you, I would say the problem now is getting him to part with Sister's fob watch.'

Somehow, with a little bribery and persuasion, they achieved it and as the boy toddled off with his mother in a flurry of hand-waving and goodbyes Nick turned to Helen.

'You looked great,' he said softly, 'cuddled in with that little mite.'

She flushed. 'You weren't doing so bad yourself,' she replied.

'I love kids,' he said huskily. 'I think they're just great.'

'Even when they're screaming?'

He nodded. 'Even when they're screaming.' Gently he reached out and with one hand took a strand of her hair that the child had pulled loose and tucked it back into her cap. With a wink he moved out of the cubicle to return to the growing chaos in the treatment rooms, leaving Helen alone.

She should have followed him but she didn't, standing instead for a moment and thoughtfully fingering her fob watch.

The incident with the child had been just one of many, typical of hundreds of others on any day in A and E, but somehow it had been different. Something had happened during that incident, either when she had seen Nick with his dark head next to the fair one of the child's or when the child had reached out, touched her watch and miraculously stopped crying.

She wasn't sure when it had happened or even quite

what had happened. She only knew that something had clarified in her mind to such an extent that now, quite suddenly, she knew exactly what it was she had to do.

When her shift was over she made her way into Reception to wait for Nick. He appeared almost immediately, struggling into his leather jacket.

'I've just had a call from the garage,' he said. 'The car I ordered has apparently arrived.'

'I'll run you over there on the way home,' said Helen, 'then you can pick it up.' She felt a slight pang as she said it. This meant they would no longer travel to and from work together, which was slightly ludicrous when she recalled how against them travelling together she had been in the first place.

'Thanks,' he said. 'That's kind. It's a bit out of your way. I hope it won't make you too late, getting home.'

'That's OK,' Helen replied. 'I do have to go out...but it'll be all right.' She didn't tell him where she proposed to go.

'You can just drop me off,' he said as they went outside. 'It'll take me a little while to complete the paperwork.'

It was still daylight and the wind was high, tossing the evergreens behind the hospital and whirling leaves up into the air. A little later when they took the coast road the surf was mountainous with huge breakers rolling in, foaming and pounding the sea defences to send spray shooting high into the air and cascading across the road.

'What a fabulous sight that is,' said Helen. 'Nature in all her different moods never fails to move me.'

'Nor me,' Nick agreed. Then with a sigh, he said, 'But it takes a lot, you know, to beat a Norfolk sunset.' As Helen threw him a sidelong glance he chuckled.

He was still smiling when she dropped him off at the garage. She wound down the window as he walked around to her side of the car, battling against the wind.

'Will I see you later?' he said. He spoke casually but she detected the curiosity beneath the question.

'You may do,' she replied, equally as casual. 'It depends what time I get back.'

'Are you going home before you go to wherever it is you're going?'

'Yes. I have to see to Chester first.'

'Oh, yes, of course.' He paused. 'Well, I'd best be off, then.'

'All right, Nick.' As he turned to go into the garage the wind caught his hair, whipping it across his face, and suddenly as she watched him Helen found her heart was bursting with love.

She felt curiously detached as she drove home. Now that her decision had been made a calmness had settled over her, a calmness which was at odds with the ferocity of the elements but which had nevertheless brought a stillness to her soul that had been missing in the last few weeks.

It was almost dusk by the time she reached the Coach House, and although the wind howled and whistled through the conifers Chester's welcoming bark was still audible. She shut the car door and hurried into the house, battling against the force of the wind.

She greeted Chester and let him out into the garden to forage around. Then she hurried upstairs to her bedroom, where she took off the clothes she'd worn for work and pulled on a comfortable pair of cords and a warm chenille sweater.

Minutes later she returned to the kitchen, opened the back door for Chester, who streaked past her, and was just putting his meal into his feeding bowl when she was surprised to hear the sound of a car on the drive, its tyres crunching on the loose gravel.

'Goodness,' she said, half to Chester and half to herself. 'Nick's home already. That was quick.' Leaving a disinterested Chester, whose main priority at that moment was his dinner, she hurried through to the hall just as the doorbell sounded.

'My word,' she said with a laugh as she tugged open the door. 'I didn't expect you yet, Nick...' Then the words died on her lips for the man standing on the doorstep wasn't Nick at all.

'Sorry to disappoint you,' he said, 'but it isn't Nick—it's me. Can I come in?' With a quizzical smile on his face Richard Fleetwood stepped across the threshold and into the hall.

CHAPTER TWELVE

'RICHARD.' She stared at him. 'I was just coming to see you.'

'So I've saved you a journey.' He closed the front door behind him, gave her a perfunctory kiss on the cheek and followed her down the passage to the kitchen.

She frowned. There was something in the way he'd spoken, something in the tone of his voice, that just for a moment made her wonder about the nature of this visit. Chester, replete after his dinner, just about managed a welcome, before crashing out on the rug in front of the Aga.

'Would you like some tea, coffee or...or a lager or something?' she asked hesitantly, still uncertain what he wanted.

'Later, perhaps.' He waved a dismissive hand, prowled around the kitchen a couple of times then sat down at the pine table. 'But first, Helen, I think we should talk.'

'Oh.' Slowly she sank onto another chair, facing him across the table.

He came straight to the point. 'I've had a visit,' he said.

'A visit?'

'Yes,' he replied, 'from Kate.'

Helen swallowed and gave a nervous little laugh. 'Isn't that a little strange when you work with each other all day?'

'Not really.' Richard shrugged. 'Work is work—this visit was personal.'

'Oh, I see.' Her mind raced ahead as she tried to imagine exactly what Kate might have told him. Richard's expression, however, gave nothing away and she soon gave up the attempt.

'Helen, you and I have been friends,' he went on, 'close friends, for a very long time...yes?'

'Yes.' She nodded. 'Yes, of course.'

'I would go so far as to say that I don't think we've ever had occasion to lie to one another. Would you agree with that?'

She nodded, her mind briefly slipping back to the time he had married Diana and she'd had to pretend she was ecstatically happy for them. But that didn't exactly constitute a lie and, therefore, probably didn't count.

'So,' Richard went on, 'I want you to be absolutely straight with me now.'

'OK.' She nodded, aware that her heart was thumping harder than was probably good for it.

'Do you love me, Helen?' he asked bluntly.

She stared at him—at the tall figure, the receding hairline, the warm brown eyes and the kind smile. Yes, she did love him. Had always loved him. For as long as she could remember she had loved Richard Fleetwood. And no doubt he knew that so there was no use pretending otherwise. 'Yes, Richard,' she said at last. 'I do love you. And I think I always will.'

'Good,' he said, 'so we've established that. I love you too, Helen. You are my dearest friend. I doubt anyone could have got me through the last few years as well as you have. I hope also I've been there for you when you've needed someone.' He raised his eyebrows and when she nodded he went on, 'As far as I'm concerned, nothing in this world can ever change that. Do you agree?'

'Of course…'

'Right,' he said almost briskly. 'So far so good. Now, I have another question for you.' Leaning his elbows on the table, he made a steeple with his hands and stared intently at her over the top. 'Do you,' he said, 'love Nick Sawyer?'

She continued to stare at him, taken aback by the directness of the question. He wanted an answer and it was then that she was forced to look away, afraid of the pain she might be about to see in his eyes.

'Helen…?' he prompted after a moment, and lowered his head slightly, trying to force her to meet his gaze again.

She took a deep breath. 'Yes,' she admitted, 'I do.'

'Ah,' he said, and there was a wealth of understanding in the single word.

'Richard, I…' Helplessly she stretched out her hand across the table but, appearing not to notice, he leaned back in his chair and carried on talking.

'So,' he said, 'we now have a situation where you love both me and Nick Sawyer. Would you say the love you feel for each of us was the same?'

She remained silent for a long moment then she shook her head. 'No, Richard,' she said at last, allowing her gaze to meet his again, 'it isn't the same. I can't explain it, but it isn't the same…'

'Would you like me to try to explain what I think you might feel for Nick Sawyer?'

'If you like.' She gave a helpless little shrug, wondering just where this rather bizarre conversation was leading. This was not what she had intended at all.

'I think,' said Richard quietly, 'that what you feel for Nick is what I felt for Diana.'

She caught her breath. 'Diana?'

He nodded. 'You say you love me, Helen, but that what you feel for me is different to what you feel for Nick Sawyer. You didn't know that difference before because you'd never actually been *in* love before. I knew the difference because I'd been *in* love—with Diana. I also knew you weren't *in* love with me.'

'Any more than you were *in* love with me,' she said quietly.

He spread his hands, the gesture apologetic yet at the same time an acceptance of the inevitable.

'If I'm honest,' he said after a moment, 'I doubt I am over Diana yet.'

She threw him a sharp glance, remembering all the mementoes of Diana at Fleetwood House—the photographs, her clothes, her possessions that should have long gone.

'I dare say I probably should be over losing her by now,' he said, looking up, catching Helen's eye and giving a slight shrug, 'but I have to work through things in my own time. I'm coming out of it,' he said quickly when Helen would have intervened, 'but sometimes…well…sometimes I doubt I will ever marry again. Don't get me wrong,' he said hastily, 'that isn't a sob story. I'm not looking for sympathy or feeling hard done by, it's simply the way things are. I have the children. The difficult teen years are ahead—heaven help us—and then, who knows, maybe one day…?' He trailed off and shrugged again.

A moment later he said, 'That's another thing. Children. I have my family, but you, well, you should have children of your own, Helen.'

He lapsed into silence again and the only sounds to be heard in the kitchen were the ticking of the old wall clock, the odd snore from Chester and, from outside, the roar of the wind.

'What did Kate tell you?' asked Helen after a while.

'She told me that, whether or not I was aware of the fact, I was being very selfish. She told me bluntly that it appeared to the outside world that I was stringing you along. She told me that Nick Sawyer was in love with you and she believed that you felt the same way about him, but you were afraid of hurting me.'

'I was,' Helen agreed. 'I dreaded telling you, Richard. I felt you'd been through enough and I didn't want to be responsible for adding to your burden.'

'Well, you can forget that,' he said gently. It was his turn to stretch his hand out across the table and take hers. 'You won't add to my burden, as you put it, provided...'

'Yes?' she said quickly.

'That we always remain friends.' As he spoke he squeezed her hand.

'We will,' she said, her gaze directly meeting his. 'Of course we will. Nothing can change that.'

Richard sighed, smiled then lowered his head as if in relief. A moment later he looked up again and said, 'So, what will happen?'

'What do you mean?' Her hand still rested in his and a strange feeling was beginning to flood through her veins, a feeling which at first she failed to recognise but which she gradually came to realise was relief.

'Will Nick Sawyer stay at the Shalbrooke?'

'Oh,' said Helen, withdrawing her hand at last and sitting up straight. 'I see what you mean. No.' She shook her head. 'He plans to return to his home in Norfolk and go into the practice that his late father founded.'

'And he wants you to go with him?' Richard raised his eyebrows.

Helen nodded.

'Now that I'm not sure I can stand,' said Richard. 'The thought of you leaving the Island is something I never contemplated, I have to confess.'

'I shall miss the Island,' said Helen. 'I don't doubt that. I am, after all, an Islander through and through, but...maybe it's time to move on and make a fresh start. My roots may be here, but I no longer have any ties, apart...' she glanced over her shoulder '...from you, of course, old chap,' she said, as Chester's tail thumped the floor as a reminder.

'That's a point,' said Richard. 'What about Chester?'

Helen smiled. 'Wherever I go, Chester goes, too.'

'So there's little more to say.' Richard stood up and as he moved around the table Helen also rose. 'Except, that is...' he looked down at her '...for me to wish you all the luck in the world. Nick Sawyer is a very lucky man and I have to confess to feeling rather envious and wishing that it could have been like that for us. He'd better love you and cherish you, Helen, because if he doesn't he'll have me to answer to.' Lowering his head he very gently kissed her mouth. Straightening up, he said gruffly, 'I think I'd better go before I start getting too sentimental and disgracing myself.'

When they reached the hall Helen opened the front door and they stood for a moment, watching the trees toss about in the wind. Glancing across at the dark outline of the stable block, Richard said, 'Where is he tonight?'

'He isn't home yet,' Helen replied.

'No doubt he won't be long,' replied Richard.

'No…' Helen paused. 'And when he gets here I think it will be time to set a few matters straight.'

'Really?' Richard looked a little surprised. 'And why is that?'

'Well,' said Helen, 'it seems everyone else knows about my feelings, my intentions and what is or isn't good for me. I think it's high time that Nick knew as well, don't you?'

'Oh, absolutely,' said Richard solemnly. With a chuckle and a wave he was gone—out of the house, into his car and away down the drive.

With a little sigh Helen turned and went back into the house. The feeling of relief that she had experienced earlier when she had realised that she and Richard could part amicably and still remain friends was now tinged with some other emotion—a feeling dangerously laced with excitement. But she had no time to examine that emotion or, indeed, any other for no sooner had the sound of Richard's car died away than it was replaced by the sound of another car that crunched to a halt on the forecourt.

Helen stopped and listened, then, with her heart thudding so hard she feared it might burst, she ran back to open the front door and almost hurled herself into Nick's arms, winding her arms around his neck and pressing her lips against his, while he stood there in amazement.

'Well,' he said at last when they drew apart, 'I shall have to buy a new car more often if it brings on this sort of reaction.'

'Oh,' she said, 'I'd quite forgotten about the car. Is it all right?'

'Yes.' He looked bemused. 'It's fine. Do you want to see it?'

'Of course. But not now,' she added quickly as he would have turned back to the door. 'Later, Nick. First, I want to talk to you.' Taking his hand, she led him through the house, not to the kitchen where she had sat with Richard but to the cosy sitting room at the back of the house with its chintz furnishings and thick velvet curtains.

'Was that Richard's car I passed in the lane?' he said curiously as she closed the door behind them.

'Yes,' she replied quickly. 'Yes, it was. It was strange because I had planned to go and see him this evening.'

'Oh, really?' Nick sounded a little cool. 'So that was where you were going?'

'Yes.' She nodded. 'He saved me the journey.'

'So, what was it all about?' Nick looked wary but mystified as she took his hand and drew him down beside her onto the sofa.

'It was about us, my darling,' she said.

'You mean you told him?' His eyes widened with surprise but also with the first glimmerings of delight.

'Yes,' she said. 'I told him, but I think I was only confirming what he already knew.'

'But how did he know?'

'Apparently, Kate had told him.'

'Kate?'

'Yes, it seems Kate wasn't prepared to stand by and let me deny my love for you.'

'So Kate knew?'

'Oh, yes,' she said ruefully. 'Kate knew. There isn't much that gets past her, you know. Anyway, she told Richard.'

'But what exactly did she tell him?'

'That she suspected we loved each other but that she feared I would let you go because of loyalty to him...'

'And would you have done that?' he murmured softly.

'No,' she said, looking steadily at him. 'No, Nick, I wouldn't. That was why I was going to see Richard tonight, to tell him that I love you and that my relationship with him was at an end.'

'Do you really mean that?' Leaning towards her, he reached out, took her chin and tilted it so that he could look into her eyes.

'Yes, Nick.' She gazed steadily back at him. 'I do.'

'Helen,' he murmured, his voice catching in his throat as he lowered his head.

They were silent for a long moment as each came to terms with this new situation, then Nick looked up again and said, 'How did he take it?'

'Quite well,' she replied. With a little frown, she added, 'Actually, I think you might have been right when you said there was something wrong with our relationship. You see, he hasn't really got over Diana—'

'I suspected that—' Nick began.

But, not giving him the chance to say more, Helen rushed on, 'He didn't love me, you know, not really.'

'Helen, I'm sorry…'

'No, Nick, don't be. There's no need. Honestly. When I say he didn't love me, what I mean is that he didn't love me in the way you love me or in the way he loved Diana. He loved me as a friend, a very dear friend, but I don't think it was ever much more than that. Diana was the real love of his life and I doubt he'll find anything like that again, and even if he does I don't think it will be for a very long time.'

There was silence for a moment then quietly Nick said, 'And what about you, Helen? What about your love for Richard?'

'I loved him once,' she said honestly. 'But that was

young love—first love, if you like. I lost him to Diana, and after she died I suppose I thought it could be rekindled. But I was wrong, wrong on two counts. One, because Richard had never been in love with me, anyway, and the other because I had changed. I had matured and I now know that whatever it is I feel for Richard it isn't the same as I feel for you. I'm *in* love with you, Nick. I merely love Richard, and that's the difference.'

'Do I get the incredible feeling that all this is leading somewhere?' Nick gave a chuckle deep in his throat and leaned back against the sofa.

'You asked me to marry you,' said Helen softly.

'Yes,' he agreed. 'I did.'

'But did you mean it? Were you sure?' For one moment she was almost afraid to look at him, afraid that she might have dreamt it or, worse, that he hadn't meant what he'd said or even that he might have changed his mind.

He was silent for a long, tense moment, as if choosing his words with care, while Helen anxiously scrutinised his face, the face that had become so dear to her in such a short space of time. If he told her it had all been a mistake she doubted whether she could bear it because never in her life had she felt this way about another human being. Even Richard, in the early days, hadn't evoked feelings like this.

At last he spoke, leaning towards her as he did so, taking her face between his hands and gazing deeply into her eyes. 'I've never been more sure of anything in my life,' he said. 'I knew the moment I saw you that you were the woman I wanted to spend the rest of my life with. The time we spent together in London proved it, if I needed any proof. Now the time I've spent with you here has only convinced me all the more. I love you,

Helen, you love me, and there's nothing now that can keep us apart.' He paused. 'The only doubts I still have…'

'Yes?' she said quickly, anxiously.

'Is how you will adapt to the life of a GP's wife in rural Norfolk.'

'If that is your only concern you can stop worrying because quite honestly, Nick, I can hardly wait.'

He laughed and quickly kissed her mouth, then her cheeks, her eyelids and finally the tip of her nose. 'Restrain yourself, woman.' A more solemn light came into his eyes and he said, 'Seriously, if you want to continue with your career, Helen, I won't stand in your way.'

'We'll see,' she said with a smile. 'I may find that I shall want to put the career bit on hold for a while and concentrate on being a wife.'

She stood up and, taking his hand, led him out of the room, into the hall and up the stairs. Her bedroom was at the end of a long passage that ran right across the back of the house, and without a trace of hesitation she led him inside.

But then it was he who took control. He who lit the small lamp beside the bed and he who undressed her, carefully, thoughtfully, almost reverently, removing every garment and draping it over the back of the Victorian chair in the corner.

When she was quite naked he lifted her into his arms and carried her to the bed where she sank into the soft down of quilt and pillows and, aching with desire, watched as he removed his own clothes.

How many times since London had she dreamed of this moment—despaired of it ever happening again? Now at last it was happening, it was real.

She opened her arms to him and he came to her,

stretching above her, caressing and loving her with words and touch, arousing with fingertips and tongue sensations she'd thought would remain only memories.

And when finally he took her in a rush of passion it was as inevitable, as natural, as the opening of a flower or the setting of the sun.

What they had started in London, that journey of wonder and desire, they continued far into the night, bringing each other time and again to sweet fulfilment as they explored, recognised and understood each others' needs and desires and how to satisfy them.

And when at last they slept it was warm and safe in each other's arms, and they were oblivious to the gales that still raged outside.

Helen woke first, in that first instant wondering what had happened, until with a surge of love she remembered and turned her head to look at the man who still slept beside her.

Dark hair was tousled on the cream lace of the pillow and dark lashes brushed his cheeks, still tanned from foreign sun.

Nick had been concerned about her leaving her island to go to the wide spaces of rural Norfolk, but would he not also miss those far-flung regions he had come to love so much? This would be a new beginning for them both. There would probably be protests from her friends and colleagues about her leaving, not only the Shalbrooke but also the Island. Helen had no doubts for never before in her entire life had anything felt more right.

Slowly, so as not to awaken him, she turned her head towards the window. There was a stillness outside; the gales of the previous night had abated and the only sound to be heard now was the repetitive call of a wood-pigeon.

Pale sunshine filtered through the curtains, spilling across the polished wooden floor and highlighting their clothes on the chair.

Her thoughts turned to Richard and once again she felt an almost overwhelming sense of relief that she hadn't hurt him and that they would still be friends. She hoped that one day he would find someone else to share his life, but maybe that wasn't meant to be. Maybe the love he'd shared with Diana, short though it had been, was enough to sustain him for a lifetime.

'I hope you're not lying there having second thoughts.'

Swiftly she turned her head to find that not only was Nick awake but, propped on one elbow, he was watching her. 'Of course not,' she said. 'How could you think such a thing?'

'I never take anything for granted,' he said. 'Let's face it, last time we were in this situation I woke up to find that you'd gone.'

'That will never happen again,' she said softly. 'I can promise you that. Besides, that was then, in London. Everything has changed now.' She paused, studying his face with the morning shadow of growth around his jaw. 'But, talking of London, there is just one thing that is bothering me.'

'Oh, yes?' he said, lazily innocent. 'And what's that?'

'Just how did you come to be at that conference?'

'Coincidence?' His eyes widened slightly.

'I was almost prepared to believe that at the time,' she said.

'But not now, is that it?' He raised his eyebrows and she noticed the gleam of amusement in his eyes and the beginnings of a smile, lurking around the corners of his mouth.

'No, not now.'

'And why is that?'

'Mainly because of something that you said yesterday.'

'Go on.' He settled himself more comfortably against the pillows. 'I'm intrigued.'

'You said that you knew from the moment you saw me that I was the woman for you.'

'Yes?'

'Well, the moment you first saw me was at Kate's and Jon's wedding and, knowing you as I do now, if that was the case then I can't imagine you leaving it there.'

'So what do you think I would have done about it?'

'I'm not sure...but something...'

'You mean like find out where you were going to be and when?' he asked softly.

'Is that what you did?' She sat up in bed and stared down at him. 'You mean you actually found out that I was going to be there at that conference?'

When he didn't reply she said, 'But how? How did you find out?'

'It's not *what* you know in this life, my love, it's *who* you know,' he said with a grin.

'But who? I still don't understand.' She looked bewildered.

'I have friends, too, you know.'

'Friends?' She stared at him. 'You don't mean Jon...and Kate?'

'No, it wasn't Kate,' he said, 'but I guess it's time I came clean. Yes, it was Jon who tipped me off.'

Still she stared at him, utterly speechless now she realised that what she had thought a delightful coincidence had been nothing of the sort.

'You mustn't blame Jon,' said Nick, and at last he had the grace to look a little shamefaced. 'I pestered him constantly, you see. I was desperate to see you again.'

'Well!' she said at last. 'Honestly. And to think in the past it's been me who has been labelled a matchmaker. Now it seems they've all had a go at arranging things for me—Jon, Kate, who gave me a good talking to then went to see Richard. Even Georgina has had her say…'

'Actually,' said Nick with a grin, 'seeing it's confession time, there is one other small thing…'

'Go on,' she said with an exaggerated sigh, 'what is it?'

'It's about me moving into the flat…'

'Yes?'

'Well, that was also engineered by Jon…and Kate, I'm afraid.'

'Oh, she was in on it as well by then, was she?'

'I'm afraid so. I don't think she and Jon have too many secrets from each other.'

'But…' Helen frowned '…if I remember rightly, wasn't it Richard who first suggested you renting the flat?'

'Yes,' Nick agreed. 'It was, but Kate had apparently already put the idea in his mind so when I said I was looking for somewhere to live…'

'I'm amazed she didn't feel guilty about Richard. She is his partner, for heaven's sake!'

'She told me she hadn't been happy about the two of you for a long time,' said Nick, growing serious again. 'She felt your relationship was drifting and wouldn't come to anything,' he went on. 'So when I came along, declaring undying love for you, she decided to help things along a bit.'

'Well!' said Helen, suddenly speechless at the sheer amount of subterfuge that had been going on.

'Do you have any complaints?' asked Nick, reaching up and drawing her down again beside him on the pillow.

'Of course not,' she admitted with a rueful laugh. 'How could I?' She gave a deep sigh then said reluctantly, 'But I'm not sure we have time for this now, you know.'

'Yes, we have,' he replied, moving so that once again his body covered hers. 'We are both on the late shift today—we have plenty of time.'

'There's something I have to do on the way to work—' she began.

'Wherever it is, there's still time for this,' he said, as he silenced her with a kiss.

The gales had torn whole branches from trees, and twigs and piles of soggy leaves littered the roads, but, mercifully, the wind had dropped when Helen and Nick later made their way to the cemetery on a wind-swept hillside above the village of Carisbrooke. Helen carried a bunch of copper chrysanthemums in her arms.

'They were his favourite,' she said, as she stooped to arrange them in the earthenware pot sunk into the earth on the still-recent grave, 'and today would have been his birthday.'

'I wish I could have known him,' said Nick, bending to help her, 'but I hope he knows that in spite of the fact that I'll be taking you away from your island I will always take care of you.'

'I'm sure he does.' Helen smiled.

When she had finished arranging the flowers she stood in silent remembrance for a moment, before joining Nick who had moved a few paces away and was admiring the magnificent views.

On one side Carisbrooke Castle crouched on its hill like some great guardian lion and below them the village basked quietly in sunshine, unexpected in the aftermath of the storm. All around them the rest of the Wight stretched as far as the eye could see, to the very shores of the Solent, while beyond in the distance the mainland coastline was clearly visible.

'You will miss all this, won't you?' Nick slipped one arm around her and held her close.

'Yes,' she admitted, 'I dare say I shall. But it won't be going anywhere. We shall come back to visit everyone from time to time.'

'Will someone tend the grave for you?' Nick glanced over his shoulder.

'Yes, I'm sure Siobhan will do that,' Helen replied. 'She was very fond of her uncle Harry.'

'Speaking of Siobhan,' said Nick thoughtfully, as they turned and began to make their way down the steep path, 'weren't she and Dave one of those couples whose romance you felt partly responsible for, along with Kate and Jon, and Georgina and Andrew?'

Helen nodded. 'Yes,' she replied, 'even if it wasn't quite what I had intended at the time.' She threw him a quick glance. 'Why do you ask?'

'I was just thinking,' he said, with a sudden chuckle. 'I guess Siobhan was about the only one who didn't play any part in trying to get us together—it seems all the others had a go.'

'That's true,' Helen agreed, with a laugh, then she paused. 'But, actually, you know,' she went on after a moment, 'Siobhan did play a part, although she was not aware of it.'

'Really?' he said. 'And what was that?'

'Well,' she said slowly, 'it was when she told me she was expecting a baby. I can't really explain it, Nick, but I had the most extraordinary feelings. Maybe it's what women mean when they say they're feeling broody. I don't know. But suddenly it made me realise just how much I wanted a family.'

'That doesn't present any problem, I can assure you.' Nick hugged her even closer.

'No,' she said, smiling up at him, 'I didn't for one moment think it would.'

'But before that,' he said with a laugh, 'we've got a wedding to plan. Let's go and tell the others the news.'

'Somehow I don't think it'll be that much of a surprise,' Helen replied as they opened the cemetery gate and stepped out onto the road. 'After all, it's been a year of weddings. You could say it's getting to be a habit.'

Nick laughed. 'Maybe—but I can't think of a better one, can you?'

'Oh, no.' Helen smiled and rested her head on his shoulder as they walked to the car. 'Absolutely not.'

MILLS & BOON®

Medical Romance™

COMING NEXT MONTH

EMERGENCY by Christine Adams

Dr Sherrie Walker was second choice for the job in A&E, so she was touchy with her boss, consultant Tim O'Neill. It also seemed he had a partner, though he didn't act like it, particularly with Sherrie!

THE PRACTICE WIFE by Margaret O'Neill

Moving from London to Cornwall, Maggie immediately felt at home, but as she began to get more involved with Dr Stewart Trelawney's personal life, she wondered whether it was just the place she loved.

THE FAMILY FRIEND by Gill Sanderson
Book 3 in the Loving Sisters trilogy

Youngest sister Rosalind was used to fighting for what she wanted, and Mark was to be no exception; he was funny *and* gorgeous! He was also her boss and a lot older, and he wasn't at all sure they should be involved.

A LITTLE IMMEDIATE CARE by Carol Wood

District Nurse Holly had to include new locum Dr Reece Caine on her house visits. Although both were reluctant to get involved, the attraction between them was potent! But he was only there for six months...

Available at most branches of WH Smith, Tesco, Asda, Martins, Borders and all good paperback bookshops

Your Special Christmas Gift

Three romance novels from Mills & Boon® to
unwind with at your leisure—
and a luxurious Le Jardin bath gelée to pamper
you and gently wash your cares away.

for just £5.99

Featuring
Carole Mortimer—Married by Christmas
Betty Neels—A Winter Love Story
Jo Leigh—One Wicked Night

MILLS & BOON®

Makes your Christmas time special

Available from 23rd October 1998

CHRISTMAS

Affairs

MORE THAN JUST KISSES UNDER THE MISTLETOE...

Enjoy three sparkling seasonal romances by your
favourite authors from

MILLS & BOON®
Presents™

HELEN BIANCHIN
For Anique, the season of goodwill has become...
The Seduction Season

SANDRA MARTON
Can Santa weave a spot of Christmas magic for Nick
and Holly in... *A Miracle on Christmas Eve?*

SHARON KENDRICK
Will Aleck and Clemmie have a... *Yuletide Reunion?*

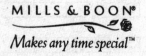

MILLS & BOON®

Makes any time special™

Available from 6th November 1998

FIND THE FRUIT!

How would you like to win a year's supply of Mills & Boon® Books—FREE! Well, if you know your fruit, then you're already one step ahead when it comes to completing this competition, because all the answers are fruit! Simply decipher the code to find the names of ten fruit, complete the coupon overleaf and send it to us by 30th April 1999. The first five correct entries will each win a year's subscription to the Mills & Boon series of their choice. What could be easier?

A	B	C	D	E	F	G	H	I
15					20			
J	**K**	**L**	**M**	**N**	**O**	**P**	**Q**	**R**
	25						5	
S	**T**	**U**	**V**	**W**	**X**	**Y**	**Z**	
			10					

4	19	15	17	22

15	10	3	17	15	18	3

2	19	17	8	15	6	23	2	19

4	19	15	6

4	26	9	1

7	8	6	15	11	16	19	6	13

3	6	15	2	21	19

15	4	4	26	19

1	15	2	21	3

16	15	2	15	2	15

C8J

Please turn over for details of how to enter ➜

HOW TO ENTER

There are ten coded words listed overleaf, which when decoded each spell the name of a fruit. There is also a grid which contains each letter of the alphabet and a number has been provided under some of the letters. All you have to do, is complete the grid, by working out which number corresponds with each letter of the alphabet. When you have done this, you will be able to decipher the coded words to discover the names of the ten fruit! As you decipher each code, write the name of the fruit in the space provided, then fill in the coupon below, pop this page into an envelope and post it today. Don't forget you could win a year's supply of Mills & Boon® Books—you don't even need to pay for a stamp!

Mills & Boon Find the Fruit Competition
FREEPOST CN81, Croydon, Surrey, CR9 3WZ
EIRE readers: (please affix stamp) PO Box 4546, Dublin 24.

Please tick the series you would like to receive if you are one of the lucky winners

Presents™ ❏　Enchanted™ ❏　Medical Romance™ ❏
Historical Romance™ ❏　Temptation® ❏

Are you a Reader Service™ subscriber?　　Yes ❏　　No ❏

Ms/Mrs/Miss/Mr ....Initials ....
　　　　　　　　　　　　　　　　　　(BLOCK CAPITALS PLEASE)

Surname..

Address ....

....

...........................Postcode..........................

(I am over 18 years of age)

C8J

mps
MAILING
PREFERENCE
SERVICE